Penguin Books
The Disappearance

Derek Marlowe was born in London in 1938. He was sent
down from London University for a controversial article in
his college magazine, and for a while took up acting. In 1960
he wrote a play, *The Seven Who Were Hanged,* which was
performed at the Edinburgh Festival and then transferred to
the Royal Court as *The Scarecrow* in 1961. This won the
Foyle Award for the Best New Play of that year. In 1962
he adapted *Lower Depths* for the Royal Shakespeare Company.
Two years later he went to Berlin on a Ford Foundation
Grant and wrote two plays which were performed there and
at the Questors Theatre. He also won an American 'Emmy'
for the television series, *The Search for the Nile.* In 1965 he
wrote his first novel *A Dandy in Aspic,* which achieved
immediate success. It has been published in fifteen countries
and made into a film (with Laurence Harvey and Mia
Farrow) for which he wrote the screenplay. His other novels
include *The Memoirs of a Venus Lackey* (1968), *A Single
Summer with L.B.* (1969), *Do You Remember England?*
(1972), *Somebody's Sister* (1974) and *Nightshade* (1976)

Derek Marlowe

The Disappearance

Penguin Books

Penguin Books Ltd, Harmondsworth,
Middlesex, England
Penguin Books, 625 Madison Avenue,
New York, New York 10022, U.S.A.
Penguin Books Australia Ltd, Ringwood,
Victoria, Australia
Penguin Books Canada Ltd, 2801 John Street,
Markham, Ontario, Canada L3R 1B4
Penguin Books (N.Z.) Ltd,
182–190 Wairau Road,
Auckland 10, New Zealand

First published as *Echoes of Celandine* by Jonathan Cape 1970
Published in Penguin Books 1973
Reissued under the present title 1977

Made and printed in Great Britain by
Richard Clay (The Chaucer Press) Ltd,
Bungay, Suffolk
Set in Linotype Granjon

Contents

To my children

Acknowledgements

The verse quoted in the novel is by Hart Crane, unless otherwise stated, and is used by kind permission of Oxford University Press.

The lines from 'Prose of the Trans-Siberian' by Blaise Cendrars (translated by Walter Albert) are reproduced by permission of Peter Owen Ltd.

The lines from 'Morning Glory' by Tim Buckley and Larry Beckett are quoted by permission of Third Story Music Inc.

Part One *Artifact*

1. False Braye

Within a single hour her absence was opaque. There were no more abstractions. I tread unexpectedly on her comb, shiver, and realize she has left me a single blonde hair the length of a crochet needle. Thoughts shatter my controlled routine, popping up startled before me like pheasants disturbed in the undergrowth as I resolve to return her books (unread) to the library, and plunder through the daily mundanity alone. A crossword puzzle half completed by her is completed by me and stored as always to await tomorrow's betrayals. No more abstractions, a Scrabble board perhaps is required to assess the reality. Images: a treasured portrait removed from the wall after nine years (*nine* years? Can it be that long?) dominating the room no longer with its colours but with the void. No more abstractions, of course; mere poultices to one's ego, bolstering one's relief that she has gone at last. Inevitable. *Her calls, her enthusiasms* ... The tenth year will be bliss, alone, uncluttered by her. A peony may be placed in a vase, a pentameter dithered out on a wet Friday afternoon, but there are no regrets. She has gone, I move around the perimeter of her recent presence, brushed by the velvet sleeves of her departing existence, and discover almost too casually (head turning away, hand reaching for a cuff-link) that her suitcase (red and brown) has deserted me too, exchanging its place on a shelf for a chasm the size of a coach and four.

And so I daydream and invent a story, play patience, close the shutters and cease to be.

*

Entering the bed to sleep, I discover her white cotton nightdress still neatly folded under the adjacent pillow. It has been cleaned, alas, handled only by launderers, allowing me not even yesterday's fragrance of her. By her bedside, a clock, an ashtray, *The Bell Jar*, three pennies, a wedding ring, the brown cylinder of a half-eaten pippin, a single Carmen roller, a book-match. No note, of course. That would already have been mentioned, for you see I am balancing (precariously balancing, but remember I am shunning a net), balancing my own mosaic of nine years with only a polite genuflection to reality. Life must go on – not *my* life, necessarily, but hers – and wherever she is (let's plump for Bognor) I trust she'll be very happy, whoever she's with. *I* am. I have my job, my health – some of it – and a fine collection of Arthur Rackham white *deluxe* (ploughed fields, grotesque trees, hobgoblins and those pink-bottomed girls the Victorians – and myself, come to that – were so fond of) buttering my library shelves. I have also a penchant for vintage-car kits, which might surprise you. It ought to, because it surprises me. For example, I have constructed the 1929 Mercedes Benz SSK three times, which, in my book, is enough to lock anyone up.

I have also, of course, a freelance profession, disquieting and clandestine, that I chose as a beggar and which now haunts me to distraction. At the beginning I never questioned such a career, accepting it with the same bland gratitude as a demob suit; but lately there have been nightmares, sudden awakenings face down on the floor, her hand on my shoulder, guiding me back into a bed that now seems as vast and as empty as a Sunday quadrangle. *Her calls, her enthusiasms ...*

Entering the bathroom, I see a smooth disc of white amid the dust on the sill, where an object (hers?) has been removed. A bottle? A vase? Its very familiarity contorts my mind as I stand in pyjamas re-running the million visits in a vain attempt to sketch in that invisible object on the sill. I am reminded of childhood annuals containing landscapes in which the artist had hidden a gallimaufry of fetishes (a boot, two rabbits, Rover) which had to be gleefully discovered in the foliage or behind the cowshed. My success then was legendary, but no longer – the bathroom sill persists in its secret and there are no clues. I must have overlooked the object at least twice a day (a statue? No, not here. Not in a bathroom), picked it up perhaps (in one hand or two?) or moved it aside to seek out the soap. I think of colours, metals, words beginning with B – *anything* to solve a problem that is no doubt as trite and absurd as the image of myself I see reflected in the mirror. An unshaven, overweight fool staring at an empty window-sill at three o'clock in the morning in a house as silent as an urn.

Defiantly, I turn away, washing my hands of the whole affair, take two steps and am drawn back by that invisible silver thread with which mediums are so fond of lassoing their victims. A glass, perhaps, abandoned by a party guest (her lover?); and yet the diameter is too small. Six centimetres, no less. A pill-box, a coin, Gabriel's trumpet. The obsession with it is insane. Downstairs, suddenly, a telephone rings, penetrating the silence – caller imagining where I am, hurrying, hand outstretched to seize the receiver – but I ignore it. It is probably from her and I have nothing, after all, to say any more.

By six o'clock, my stomach, oblivious as usual of any ache except its own, forces me to eat. Cold chicken (ah, the cliché of it all) and olives. Then at six thirty the telephone rings again, irritatingly, like a persistent bitch waiting to be fed. I remove the receiver and leave it upside down on the blotter, impotent on its back like a tortoise. My imagery, I see, is now becoming positively maudlin, but I make no excuses. She has gone. To another bed, no doubt. I drag my imagination away from such a tableau, frightened that he might penetrate her quietness in one night when I myself failed even to *brush* her solitude after nine whole years.

Pieces fit together now. Not anecdotes, for our marriage avoided them. But bric-à-brac. A verse by Hart Crane she quoted to me once, breathless, returning late in the afternoon from a cousin's, sitting on the edge of my desk, her face in profile, assessing a scratch on her wrist while kneeing me with her sympathy.

> No more violets,
> And the year
> Broken into smoky panels.
> What woods remember now
> Her calls, her enthusiasms.

*

When I met her first, it was in a house in Bath, I believe (plastic Gothic, a child's toy cannon left out in the dark), where I had just relinquished, as is the nature of these things, another girl. A frail child, very young, with eyes the colour of malachite. Her name was Melanie (honeyed warmth in that first syllable. Milly to the Nigel she later married), whom I adored for a brief while and then abandoned for reasons I can never understand. Perhaps she had become a habit I had to break, suddenly aware that we had become a double-act to her friends (I, myself, obliged to possess none whatsoever). Melanie and Jay, consistently invited together to dinners, where, due to the absurd protocol, we were never allowed to sit together, and so endured the bovine subtlety of a publisher on her left while I (ink-blot eyes nervously surveying the arsenal of cutlery surrounding my own plate) was compelled to embroider samplers of gossip for my hostess, who, being a gourmande, decorated her stomach with portions of meat the size of a billiard pocket. When I finally left Melanie for ever, there was not one single reason I could think of to justify such irrational behaviour. I can only remember the razored scream in her eyes, and that extinct beast that came and settled in my stomach as I walked away, my back the size of a minaret.

Now Celandine had gone too. I replace the receiver on the hook and wait.

*

Nothing for eight hours. I sit in silence staring out of the window at the daily itinerary of the street. Laundry vans invariably christened after goddesses or painters (HOGARTH, for one. REMBRANDT. DIANA), except for one wretched nonconformist who brazenly embroiders one's shirts with the word GRUMBLE. Postmen, delivery boys, chauffeurs (it's that kind of neighbourhood. *Her* choice, not mine. Now, of course, only mine). A dust cart, a learner-car circling the block with the accuracy of Columbus. Model-girls denying me a glimpse of their bottoms (imagination soars), a vicar, a Buddhist monk, a rectangle of dry macadam amid the rain where a car rested. I sit in silence, untroubled.

Immobility has never bothered me, for I have learnt in my profession to endure it. I am inconspicuous (the face in the crowd is never mine) as well as being, so I have been told, totally without feeling. 'You are totally without feeling,' she once said as I cancelled the twin beds. I have no emotion. At least, not on the surface. My profession, as I have said, demands it. It is a rare calling, though lately I am beginning – her leaving like that doesn't help, God dammit. Whom can I now ignore? – to lose my touch. Age is beginning to claim its due (I am thirty-nine, have been for three months and will be for another fifty), and I am not the artist I was. I am beginning, you see, to *observe*.

For example, in the course of my life I have never seen a spectacle more ungainly than that of R., one hand still clutching the Watchet guide-book as he turned, lurched, quibbled momentarily with the rim of the cliff, then fell, head down, feet up, hat accompanying his descent like a faithful retainer, and broke into pieces on the rather pretty shingle at the base of Tintagel. For a moment, in his fall, he escaped my gaze – no doubt observing the delicacy of the granite on the way down – and then reappeared, position unchanged, to enter the ground (a slight bounce, surprisingly. Nothing too theatrical), before lying still, his limbs jigsawed out of shape on the shore.

For those of you unfamiliar with the ground plan of the castle, there is a rather unprofessional etching gummed into the rear of the official guide-book, designed I believe to be opened solely in first-class railway compartments, Gothic crypts or, failing that, Mother Hubbard's cupboard. In short, anywhere but within twenty miles of open land from the subject of the plan, for the high breezes from the Atlantic play havoc with maps, especially here on the north coast of Cornwall on a November morn.

The map itself is divided into three Wards, an acne of dotted lines representing gradients, a ditch, a gate, *two* gates and what appears to be a regiment of tadpoles. Dogs, children and that man flying the kite have been omitted from the tableau, though I remember their presence quite vividly. However, for those of you with insatiable imaginations, Man With Kite (lozenge, blue and red) was – and, no doubt, still is – positioned just south of Upper Ward, facing east and without a trilby. The children can be scattered anywhere, like confetti; as can the dogs. Except, one assumes, in the sea. Unlike R.

R. and myself are, of course, not inscribed in the brochure, unlike the false braye where we stood together, contemplating the sea and finishing off our Spam sandwiches before R. made his premature exit. And that really is all I can add, for this is hardly the time to admire the architecture, quote Malory or feed the pigeons – holding me close, she bursts into tears, hiding her head. I feel my body evaporate . . .

Another laundry van. Blue this time inscribed HAMPTON COURT above a rather pretty border of shattered lace. A woman in a felt hat studying the sky with the intensity of Turner as her poodle opens its bowels on to the kerb. An hour ago, I visited our local store and asked for a packet of Gold Leaf cigarettes. As they were being passed across the counter, I realized, sickeningly, that they were not my brand. They were Celandine's. They torment me now as they lie before me on my desk. It was a thoughtless action, but being a man of stable character, I soon overcame my mistake. Gold Leaf, you see, are fivepence cheaper than the rubbish I normally buy, which, I suppose, at a time like this is consolation enough.

＊

I am thinking of R. again as the telephone rings. Poor sod, whoever he was. Mere flotsam now at the base of Tintagel, washed by the tides, influenced by the moon, pushed by me. Three months before that, on a shy in Dorset, I almost bungled an assignment. Overpowered by a sudden, and uncharacteristic, flamboyance (it was Celandine's birthday and I was eager to return to her), I drove the victim, K. (a stockbroker, I believe, dead as mutton but warmer), across that beautiful county in order to show him the birthplace of Thomas Hardy. However, en route I was struck by the visual masterpiece of the chalk giant at Cerne Abbas, even at night, and so parked the car in a driveway at the base of the hill.

The next morning (I, by now, snoozing in bed), K.'s body was discovered by a villager (female) in the left testicle of the giant (a well of about seven feet in diameter; one of a pair) as she took her morning promenade across the enormous carving. As you probably read, the Sunday papers had a field-day over the incident, but my employers have a poor sense of humour. They disapprove of my locations, but as I tell them, no one will ever catch *me* returning to the scene of the crime. I've seen most of them before, and those I haven't, I, at least, wouldn't be seen dead in.

R. was my saving grace, but even he was too alert. Too prepared. Unlike at a bullfight, there are no picadors, you understand, to wear the opponent down before the kill. No fanfares either. No spectacle. Not even an ear. And next week, I have to erase another man; to tell you the truth I no longer have the heart for it. Especially after a situation like this. Unfortunately they have already paid me an advance of three thousand pounds and I spent that within an hour. It was on a small, jewelled brooch, circular, about six centimetres in diameter – God, *now* I remember what was on that bathroom sill. She could have left me that. That at least. Just that –

The Cerne Abbas giant, by the way, is on the A352, halfway between Sherborne and Dorchester, and is well worth a visit for the spectacle alone.

*

'You kill, Durkin, not because you want others dead, but because you want to keep yourself alive.'

'Yes, sir.'

'Now then, what will you do when this is over, Durkin? Go back to civvy street and take up a trade?'

'I thought I'd go back to being an electrician, sir. Give it a try –'

'Yes. It's a good trade. Electrician.'

'What about you, sir?'

'Leave, Durkin. Get out, before I become tarnished like the regimental silver. Let me tell you something – I may respect a general for his skill in strategy and for saving his country, but I will never respect a general for *becoming* a general. I'll leave, Durkin. Leave. Get out. There must be a job for someone of my qualifications. Something – not too dull.'

Two days after this conversation, Durkin was shot through the head while walking by the Suez Canal. That evening, the officer wrote in his journal: 'It is neither sweet nor glorious to die for one's country if one's country is neither sweet nor glorious,' and then resigned his commission. Five years later, he married Celandine. There were only the two witnesses present, no telegrams, no guests. During the honeymoon he made love to his wife only once. She was not a virgin, nor was he, nor was there any lack of desire by either party. That was just the way it was.

*

The telephone rings but I cannot answer it. Instead, I wander through the house and in a bedroom drawer discover alien objects, long forgotten, that I had never realized she had kept. A dried rose, a postcard of a painting by Alma Tadema, other postcards, a ribbon, a book of children's names unopened, a child's school cap. Letters read and returned to their envelopes. A toy trapeze-artist (wooden) bought by her in the Japanese supermarket in New York four years earlier. An Italian holy picture with a lace edge, and a poignant clipping cut from a newspaper, written by an old lady of eighty-three, reading: 'Since Penelope Noakes of Duppas Hill is gone, there is no one who will ever call me Nellie again.'

A few other things, many of which I cannot bear to list so soon after her departure; others I, regrettably, can find no cause for at all. Some lines of verse she had written herself, startling me for I had never known she had written even a syllable. I suddenly feel like a stranger, prying, without licence, into another stranger's mind, and so close the drawer carefully, and calmly leave the room. I am, as you see, in full control of my faculties: rational, stoic. Matter-of-fact. I even go down to the kitchen and make myself a drink, taking my time (the drawer forgotten), concentrating solely on measuring a whisky and soda. I take a glass, wash it, dry it, and then suddenly, quite unexpectedly, while I am removing the ice tray from the freezer, I find I have melodramatically, ridiculously, burst into tears.

*

At two thirty in the afternoon, a man who called himself Burbank came round and sat in a chair in a corner of the sitting-room, with his back to a magazine photograph of a pallid-faced girl with the mouth of a royal mistress which Celandine had pinned to the wall while I was in the Dordogne on a shy. I had returned and asked who the woman was and why she was more important than that small square of Morris wallpaper (green carnations) she had tenanted.

'It's Zelda Sayre,' she had replied, almost defiantly. 'You know? *Save Me the Waltz.* Zelda Sayre.'

'No, I don't know. Who is she?'

'Was. She's dead. She was married to F. Scott Fitzgerald.'

'Not F. Scott Fitzgerald the tree surgeon?'

'She went mad. Don't you think that's sad?'

'Yes.'

And I did. It was not as sad, say, as that book that was going to be called – and ought to have been – *The Saddest Story*, but it was sad enough. The opening line of the book was, if I recall: 'This is the saddest story I have heard.' And it is. It is. When Celandine gave it to me for my thirty-eighth birthday, inscribed: 'TO MY OWN GOOD SOLDIER. C.', I read it alone in Darlington in a single day, and finished it, terrified. It was all, without embellishment, so painfully true. And I was in Darlington. *Darlington!* When I phoned her later, at four o'clock in the morning, there was no answer. Nor at five either. Nor six.

'If I went mad, would you put *me* in a sanatorium?'

'If you wanted me to.'

'If I was mad ...' (tip of tongue appearing for a second at the corner of her mouth, to retreat immediately, point taken. Neck rising, angling from a silken collar) 'I wouldn't know what I wanted.'

'I'd put you in a sanatorium.'

'And visit me.'

'Never. But I'd put your picture on the wall.'

'Next to Zelda Sayre?'

'*Instead* of Zelda Sayre.'

Holding me close, she bursts into tears, hiding her head. I feel my body evaporate.

Burbank, I notice, smokes tipped cigarettes so I give him the packet I had bought that morning. They are thrust, they are thrust, *thrust*, into a flapless pocket. An unfussy man, fat, short, a second-billing face. His voice constantly out of synchronization with his eyes.

'I've been phoning you all day,' he tells me. 'Were you out?'

'No.'

'Why didn't you answer?'

'I thought it was my wife.'

'Your wife? I didn't know you were married.'

'I'm not any more. She left me two days ago while I was at Tintagel.'

'Why?'

'That's none of your business.'

'You brought the subject up. I don't give a damn what your private life is.'

'Good. Now we know.'

I stare at the wall for a long time and neither of us says a word for at least five minutes. I recall a story for no apparent reason: a man murders his wife in Tunbridge Wells and in order to avoid recognition he escapes to Brighton. While there, out of boredom, he takes a mystery tour and finds himself back in Tunbridge Wells. He is arrested.

'She was called Celandine,' I say quietly. 'It was the name of a great-aunt. On her mother's side, I believe.'

'When did she run away?'

'I don't think she ran. She suffered from asthma. She wouldn't run. Not her. She took her car.'

Burbank shrugs and lights another cigarette, surveys the room for an ashtray, then drops the match on the floor, avoiding my eye.

'Did you see the evening papers?' he says suddenly. 'The body of a man was washed up on the shores of Cornwall.'

'Headlines?'

'No. Page five.'

'Once I used to make headlines.'

Later it was suggested I moved into a hotel. The shy was to be in eight days. A man called Feather. I was shown a photo of him, surprised that he was so young. Pale face, thinning hair, the nose of a baccarat player. Rich apparently, married, ambitious. 'I don't want to do it,' I said, handing the photograph back. 'Not now. Not any more. Wait a while.'

'All right,' replied Burbank after a long while. 'All right. Just give us back the three thousand pounds and we'll find someone else.'

'I can't. It's all gone. I've spent it.'

. 'Feather. In eight days. He's Jewish.'

'What's that got to do with it?'

There was no reply. Then at one o'clock in the morning, Burbank went out and returned with his son's Monopoly set and a bottle of whisky.

'I'll take the shoe,' he said, 'you can have the iron.'

'I don't want anything. I want to sleep. If you get to jail, stay there.'

Exhausted, I stand up and cross to the bedroom, removing my jacket. As I am about to close the adjoining door, Burbank looks up and says casually, as if as an afterthought:

'By the way, what did you say your wife's name was?'

'Celandine. Why?'

'Nothing. It's a common enough name. Good night.'

I close the door and fall on the bed without undressing. Before I am asleep, Burbank, in the next room, has built hotels in Pall Mall, Mayfair and the Old Kent Road, as well as taking over the bank. Finally, mercifully, I close my eyes and descend into the first deep sleep for days, a sleep plagued only by a single thought – why did Burbank think that Celandine was a common enough name? My horizons may not be as wide as Marco Polo's, but I would never have thought it a common enough name. Drowsiness, however, soon takes over and questions fade. My mind becomes lead, except for a dream that I am in a car and that the car is running into a wall and that I am being crushed under the dashboard and my legs are being cut off neatly, just above my knees. On waking, of course, I realize that it is only a dream and that I am not in a car but safe in my wheelchair.

After that, I sleep, limbs intact, until almost noon, and discover that Burbank, of course, is still there. He hasn't, God help us, even taken off his tie.

2. The Hem of Melanie's Long Pink Dress

I once maintained that if there was to be an end to one's search for an identity, it would surely begin in a second-class carriage of an English train travelling west across Hampshire and Somerset to the city of Wells. There had been talk about the party for a week or more (a card had arrived and had been placed on Melanie's mantel against a carriage-clock), and preparations (new dresses, someone suddenly noticing the ominous words 'Black Tie' in the bottom right-hand corner) had commenced immediately. Four of us took the train in the afternoon, passing the time with word-games and silent observations of the passing countryside. Opposite me, Melanie, eyes lowered, long pink dress neatly folded in her suitcase above her head.

Then, Wells. A drive to the house, giggles, introductions, nervous changing into Formality in the adjacent wing and the face of Celandine appearing suddenly at a first-floor window, hair in rollers.

Later I was introduced to her by her husband, turning to me casually and gesturing towards his wife. I say nothing, leaning close towards her in the crush of the room so that I see the make-up hastily applied to red-rimmed eyes, and listen to her voice (quite a slight stammer, her mind already in the gallery), while across the room I feel Melanie's gaze bisect the guests to penetrate my back. We talk quickly, two minutes, no more, about Ingres (of all people), and then she leaves in the wake of her husband to find herself alone, among strangers. 'Looking for Michael. Have you seen him?' I hear her inquire nervously (I am now reckless) and then she walks away again, into the garden, stopping only for a brief moment at the door, to admire a child's doll held up, button-eyes missing, to be introduced.

Two yards away, Melanie lingers by a buhl cabinet, complementing its design, then quietly accepts a dance with the host, dressed like a Scarborough Proust, eyebrows semaphoring his intent as he leads her towards the music. Glancing back, she finds I have gone and allows the host to rest his hand momentarily on her bottom. I have gone, not yet in pursuit into the shrubbery, but back to the drawing-room. Unfamiliar faces, host's son, up too late and resembling a winter poodle; gossip about *her*, a Midlands peer showing snaps of Morocco to a myopic odalisque, a designer of clothes asking me about my tie. I reply politely that it had been given to me, that was all, and he smiles shyly (a likeable man whom one feels chose designing because Everest had already been conquered) and eases himself away to return, happily, to his wife. 'It was given to him. He doesn't know from where.' Books, narrowing their scope by enlarging their pages and their price, and yet I find one, surprisingly, on Ingres. A print of 'Venus Anadyomene' – nude Sally, bald except for the hair on her head, nipples the size of aspirins and a quartet of naked louts cluttering her thighs with hands, wings, mirrors and what looks like a brass snake thrust dangerously close to her pudenda. A mazarine eclipse of puppy-pink sensuality dominated by the eyes of Venus herself, thatchet, elliptical and as remote as her planet. I stare at its delicacy, then, while seeking the coffee-table it ought to adorn, I see Celandine's face once more through the drawing-room window. She stands on the lawn, not alone, but within her own entity. *She is quite naked, has no body – is too poor*. One needs air.

*

'Tell me about Feather.'
   '*Spingularu*,' replied Burbank with disgust.
   'Tell me about Feather. Is he protected?'
   'Perhaps. He's rich. Money buys protection.'
   'I want to know if he's protected. Kami-kaze went out with hair-cream.'
   'He could be in three places,' said Burbank, 'Paris, the Canaries or Argyll. It'll be in Paris or Argyll. He only goes to the Canaries in the summer.'
   'To feed the birds.'
   'Argyll in the winter.'
   'To buy his socks.'

'If you want to make jokes, wait till I'm out of the room. I have no sense of humour.'

I suddenly remember a favourite song of hers. She would play it late at night, early in the morning, after lunch. 'It's called "Morning Glory",' she would tell me for the fiftieth time.

> I lit my purest candle close to my
> Window, hoping it would catch the eye
> Of any vagabond who passed it by,
> And I waited in my fleeting house.

Singing it to herself over and over again. I never could understand that poetry in her. At times, when she was too close, it frightened me. I discovered, after I had married, that Celandine had that too.

'*You're* a joke, Burbank,' I replied. 'Do you really want me to believe that I've been selected for Feather above all others? Five years and I'm given bank managers, barbers and shoe-salesmen. Today, here, I'm assigned a millionaire, no less, who can't even decide where he wants to live. Who do you seriously want killed – him or me?'

Slowly, with careful deliberation, Burbank replaced the pieces of his son's Monopoly set into their compartments, folded the board and closed the lid, then placed the box under his arm. The game was over.

'Give us back the three thousand pounds plus two weeks' interest – that's three thousand and ten pounds – and I'll say good-bye. Burbank will not reappear before you again.'

'Who are you fooling? I know now about Feather. If he's a millionaire, why shouldn't I warn him for twice the amount?'

'You should have stayed in bed, Mallory.'

'I know. I should have stayed in bed.'

*

Quieter ... Just there. There, Jay. Chickadee is dreaming of Bosch. There, Jay. Oh, Jay, chickadee is dreaming, dreaming of Bosch.

*

'Listen to this,' Burbank said suddenly, taking a yellowing newspaper clipping from his wallet. 'I'll read it to you:

Rockford, Illinois. March 3, 1967.

Two teen-age cousins were forced to kneel against the stone wall of an isolated park pavilion last night and then were shot to death at point-blank range, police said. Police squads rushed to the area after an anonymous tipster believed to be a woman called the Winnebago County sheriff's office and told deputies where to find the bodies. 'To hell with them,' the woman shouted over the phone. 'Just let them lay there and die.'

'Doesn't that make you want to throw up, Mallory? Women . . .'

'Why did you say Celandine was a common enough name?'

'Did I?'

'Last night.'

'Last night I played Diplomacy –'

'Monopoly.'

'– last night I played Monopoly and said many things. So did you in your sleep.'

'Such as?'

'Who cares? I never eavesdrop. I'm not Emmanuel Mittleman.'

Outside the window, a London plane tree. Leafless. Beyond that, a square, another hotel. Another plane tree.

'I'll tell them to give Feather to someone else,' Burbank said finally, walking to the door. 'You'll return the money tonight.'

'Listen, Burbank . . .'

Hesitation. He glances back at the whisky, deliberates, then picks it up.

'Listen, Burbank, I spent the money on a brooch for my wife. If I had the brooch you could have the money, but I haven't got the brooch and I'm in debt to the tax man. I even owe the paper-boy.'

'So you find your wife and take the brooch back.'

'No . . .'

'Leave it to us. We'll find her. After all, it's our money if you refuse Feather.'

'Why are you giving *me* this shy? Six months ago they wanted to fire me and now – there's something wrong with the assignment, isn't there?'

Burbank didn't say a word. What could he say? He had *his*

job and at an oblique guess, I would say he was probably a Scorpio. But let that pass.

'Leave my wife alone ... Let her go.'

Burbank shrugged.

'Listen to this:

A chronic sufferer of a debilitating bone disease and an acute victim of 'Battered Child Syndrome', seven-year-old Elizabeth Pappolla died yesterday after two weeks of savage beatings by her mother and the woman's lover.

The lover-boy, unemployed laborer John Koltosky, twenty-six, allegedly admitted to the police he pummelled the under-sized child every night for two weeks because 'I enjoy beating her.' *New York Daily News*. March 14, 1964.'

'Some *Papavero*.'

'What do you collect all these for?'

'It used to be stamps. Then cigar-bands –'

'I never knew you were musical.'

'– then photographs of women's breasts cut out of magazines. I papered the door with them. A door decorated with nipples, can you beat it?'

'I wouldn't say that, but there's been a knocker on my front door for twenty years.'

'Looked like it had measles. The door. Hundreds of pink – Now Razzili. He doesn't collect anything. Not a thing. Razzili's pockets are always empty. Totally. If he was run over, they would search him, find nothing whatsoever. Not even a coin. Razzili's very careful. Buys his clothes from chain-stores, everything. Never been near a gun, uses public transport and never writes a letter, not even to his Auntie Lottie. Razzili's a remarkable man. He's forty-three and looks twenty.'

'How much is the balance you owe me if I agree?'

'Three thousand. Like we said. Minus the ten pounds.'

'I must know more about Feather.'

'Of course. I'll tell you what little I know about him. We've got two hours.'

'Two hours?' I asked, startled. 'Two hours till what?'

'I'm driving you to the airport. You take a plane to Glasgow, then a train to Argyll. But first, may I say I'm pleased you

accepted Feather. I respect your work very much. I like your
. . . style.'

I can't go through with it. Not now. Not any more. Not now
that she has gone. Let Feather live, whoever he is. Send someone else. Send Razzili. Right now, all I want to do is kill time,
not Feather, and believe me, if you groaned at that, I'm in no
mood for puns.

*

'Promise me you won't laugh, Jay, but someone at a party
yesterday said he saw you with a girl in Hastings last week. By
the memorial. He said he didn't recognize you at first but he
recognized the girl. Jay – did you hear what I said?'

'I can't listen and shave. Say it again.'

'A man at a party saw you with a girl last weekend.'

'Where?'

'Hastings.'

'Hastings, Sussex?'

'I suppose so – Yes, of course. What other Hastings is there?'

'Last weekend I was in Lincoln. Lincoln is in Lincolnshire.
When did the man tell you this lie? While he was pulling down
your knickers?'

'According to the *R.A.C. Guide and Handbook*, Lincoln is
266 miles from London, there and back. Hastings is 130 at the
most. I looked at the milometer of your car. You travelled only
131 miles. The extra mile I suppose was to park in the wood.'

'On the contrary, Celandine. The extra mile was to find a
chemist. Make of that what you will.'

'As I was saying – this man recognized the girl first. He had
met her at Martin's show.'

'Oh really? And what did he say her name was?'

'Melanie. Didn't you go to Wells with a girl called Melanie?
Remember Wells? That was where we first entered the ring.'

'I could have done. Melanie is a common enough name. May
I now ask what the name of your informant was – move out of
the light, I almost cut my nose.'

'He was not a lover, if that's what you think.'

'As you wish.'

'His name is Durkin.'

'Durkin?'

'What's the matter?'

'I used to have a batman in the army called Durkin.'

'Well, he wasn't your bloody batman.'

'No, I know it wasn't. He's dead. He was killed in Suez in 1956. We brought him back to England to be buried at Stoke Poges. I don't know why he chose Stoke Poges except that I gave him a copy of Gray when his son was born. There's a motorway near there now.'

'Was it the same Melanie, Jay?'

'In Hastings?'

'Yes.'

'Yes, I'm afraid it was.'

*

Having endured the painful experience of flying from at least half the major capital airports in the western hemisphere, I have come to the conclusion that the master-planner who designs the ribbon of motorway from the centre of the city to the airfield is probably not only as blind as Homer, but also possesses the aesthetic taste of an egg-plant. The journey, even in a Rolls, pushing past monotonous suburban houses, office-windows (secretary in profile, boss dry-shaving) and the inevitable scrapbook of neons, has all the charm of a used Kleenex; then there's the congestion, bad driving, and irate taxi-drivers whose talent for using the route as if it were their nephew's Scalectric set is upstaged only by the arrogance of that school bully of the road, the airline bus.

London, of course, is no exception. Far from it. Leaving the hotels of West Kensington, built, it appears, solely for suicides, illicit affairs and the readers of *Die Welt*, the road strikes westward, widening encouragingly to seduce the speedometer before suddenly, maliciously, narrowing into a bridle-path full fifty feet above the rooftops of Chiswick (cars scrabbling into line, a heart-tearing rash of brakelights) to become no longer a highway but a roller-coaster, ricocheting above cricket fields, shops, two boys talking at a kerb-side (one holding a bicycle) before once again descending on to a motorway as straight and fast as a javelin and inhabited by steam-rollers. On finally arriving at the airfield, the passenger, if still sober and/or alive, steps on to the tarmac with such an elation of relief that he would rush into the waiting plane even if it was christened the *Titanic*.

On this particular afternoon, however, such emotions remained dormant en route to Heathrow airport. I merely sat in the back of the Ford, next to Burbank, and listened. I had already resolved not to take the assignment with Feather for the simple reason that only a fool could fail to see that it smelt to high hell of treachery. Thirty-nine is a bad year for risks, and if there was one thing at all I had learnt about my profession it was that no one, but no one, plays trick-or-treat with money. In Los Angeles, right now, you can hire an assassin for five hundred dollars, and many people do. In Paris, last June, T. eliminated a high-ranking civil servant for a second-hand Citroën, traded it in for a Peugeot and is still as free as speech. For eliminating a man called Feather, someone is offering me six thousand pounds, and at today's prices (1967 was the lowest year yet) you could kill a president for less. What with devaluation, the state of the pound sterling and the Common Market, the operator who is putting up six thousand pounds to extinguish someone who could be pushed off a train for sixpence is either insane, eccentric or very, very dangerous. One thing I *do* know – he's not a philanthropist. Conclusion : I graciously decline the invitation, an invitation that any rational human being would run a mile from, except that this human being has allowed his wife to escape with the get-out clause, and Burbank, as he has informed me all too frequently, has neither sentiment nor a sense of humour.

We are now halfway to the airport. Five miles to go.

'I don't want to do it,' I repeat wearily. 'Get someone else.'

'We're paying you six thousand pounds. Why quibble?'

'That's what worries me. That's four times my price and I'm getting too old. Get someone else.'

'You took the three thousand. Did I see you send it back? Is there a registered letter in the post?'

'I was greedy. My wife wanted a piece of jewellery that cost five thousand pounds, so I bought it. Don't ask me why. Mother taught me never to argue with women. Besides, she thought I was having an affair with a former girlfriend.'

'Were you?'

'No, but what else could I tell her? That I went to Hastings to stick an arrow in someone's eye?'

'I thought you *shot* Kempinski.'

'You know, Burbank, you're right. You really don't have a sense of humour.'

'So you were greedy. Stay greedy. Kill Feather and get the balance. With three thousand you could even afford a divorce.'

'But why six thousand, Burbank? Tell me.'

'He's a millionaire. He's important.'

'It's just as difficult,' I reply, 'to kill a millionaire as a beggar. They both want to live.'

'Maybe we like you.'

'Nobody likes me, Burbank. Not even my wife.'

Burbank is now drinking the Scotch. Two paper cups have been found and filled with whisky. We both sit silently, sipping the drink, staring at the back of the chauffeur's head. Outside, a clock reads 5.50 but is probably fast. On the radio that afternoon they said there might be fog in the Heligoland Bight.

'I don't want to do it. Give me a week and I'll get back the money. Life is full of surprises.'

'Why now, Mallory? Why this one? Nothing ever stopped you before.'

'I suppose,' I reply wearily, staring out at the skyline, 'I suppose I'm drawing the line. Making a stand. You'd never understand, but I'm too old, too tired to carry on. Before, I had Celandine to reassure me I was ... well, needed, if you wish. Now – I'm just drawing the line. Don't you see, Burbank? I have to. We all have to at one point.'

'But what have you got to gain by it – you know what will happen to you –'

'Gain?' I smile and glance at him. He looked nervous, shy, suddenly embarrassed by the intimacy. 'There was never anything to *gain*. But, don't you understand, for the first time since leaving the army I have nothing to *lose*. Not a damn thing.'

We are now descending towards the level and the airport can be seen on our left, on the horizon. I watch a Boeing take off, fast, thrusting upwards almost perpendicular to the ground before banking high over green fields. By the time we reach the airport it will probably be over Ireland. Next to me, Burbank leans closer and his voice drops to a whisper. I smell the alcohol and notice a tag of cigarette paper stuck defiantly to his lower lip.

'Let me tell you something, Mallory. You've got to do this. Not only for yourself, but for me.'

'You're breaking my heart,' I reply and move away into the corner of the seat. 'You couldn't hustle corpses to Burke and Hare. Get yourself another job. Anything. I knew a priest like you. He served communion to the people for fifteen years, and placed the communion wafer in so many decaying mouths that one day he realized he could serve humanity better by throwing away his collar and becoming a dentist. So he did.'

It was now five fifty-seven and getting dark.

'Please . . .'

Burbank, now drunk, moves closer.

'Please . . . I understand about your wife. I know how you feel, though if *my* wife wanted to run away I'd buy her spiked shoes. But you . . . you understand. Believe me. And I'm very sorry you are obliged to . . . so soon. Well, last night for example, I'm sitting there, in the hotel, playing Monopoly on my own. Monopoly, a game for six players – it states it on the box. Me, I'm playing it on my own. Is it, you think, because I'm in a hotel? No. Is it because all my friends are on holiday or visiting their nephews in Skegness? No. You know why I play Monopoly on my own? A game for six players? Iron, shoe, ship, hat, little pieces . . . It's because I don't know five other people, Mallory, except my wife whom I hate. And my son who couldn't play Ludo. I just don't know anybody else.'

We pass a sign gesturing towards Slough and the airport. Durkin lived at Slough. Two miles.

'I'll tell you something, Mallory,' Burbank continued. 'I'll tell you something nobody knows. No one. I'm going to tell you in order to show you I understand how you feel. So that you'll realize that I'm human too.'

For a moment, Burbank hesitates, then after another cup of whisky turns towards me once more, one hand resting on the sleeve of my left arm.

'Mallory . . . You know when Cheever was arrested? You

remember? Last year, when they picked Cheever up and everybody was convinced that someone informed on him because of the money? Well ... someone did, Mallory. Someone did. Someone walked with the *Sonnambula*. It was me. I ... Oh, God ...'

There was a sudden silence and I felt, without moving my head, Burbank slide away from me, then stare, trembling, out of the window. For a moment, I gazed at the back of his head (small bald spot the size of a brooch), glanced at the chauffeur behind the partition, at the airport, now almost before us, and lit a cigarette. The sound of the match striking made Burbank turn and he looked at the action of the match to cigarette, to inhalation, to the smoke. His face was the colour of Portland cement.

'So you see, Mallory ... We're all human. Even me. And believe me, I know nothing about Feather. I'm just a runner. But what I –'

'You shouldn't have told me about Cheever.'

'Oh, I know, Mallory. But I couldn't ... You wouldn't tell anyone. I mean ... oh, Mallory –'

'I never heard,' I said coldly. 'We chattered about Greece in that minute. You said to me, "Have you been to Greece, Mallory?" And I replied, remember? "Yes, I went once to the Valley of the Butterflies in Rhodes, only it was in May and there weren't any butterflies. So I ignored the area and visited another valley that was only half as attractive. There were no butterflies there either, but then there were never claimed to be." '

'That's a nice story, Mallory. Thank you. I'll never forget this.' He smiled, almost for the first time, shyly, then added, 'By the way, the name is Walter. Walter Burbank.'

'Fine, Walter.'

'And ... I'm sorry about your wife. Is there anything I can –'

'No.'

'No ... Well, thank you anyway. I shouldn't have –'

'How old is your son, Walter?'

'My son, Mallory? Twelve. I have a photograph. You want to see it?'

'No. We're here. We're at the airport.'

The car was now in the tunnel and emerging slowly through the maze of by-paths towards the main building. Alongside, scaffolding, workmen with yellow helmets, jets, a Negro leaning against a wall staring across the runway.

At Exit 9, the Ford stopped and the chauffeur opened the nearside door for both of us to get out.

'The plane for Glasgow is farther along,' Burbank said. 'I think you ought to try there first. Take the plane to Glasgow, then a train to Argyll. I've written down the station. You'll be met.'

'Are you sure he's in Argyll?'

'No . . . but it's likely.'

Burbank then held out his hand towards me, nervously, almost with apology.

'Thanks again, for . . .'

I shrugged, shook the hand and turned away.

'I'm going upstairs to buy some magazines,' I said quickly. 'I get bored on planes.'

There was a sudden flicker of fear in Burbank's eyes, but I ignored it.

'You don't need magazines, Mallory. It's only an hour. Besides, you'll miss the plane. You haven't even checked in. You don't need magazines. They have them on the plane.'

'Just a couple of magazines,' I replied. '*Time*, *Esquire*, something like that. Whatever they have.'

I then hurried up the escalator without looking back, and before Burbank had time to follow I was in a phone booth in the corner of the main lounge. As I dialled, I saw him appear, a hundred yards away, his face flushed, pushing past the crowds feverishly and glancing anxiously up and down the hall. He then began to run from kiosk to kiosk, at one point knocking down a child with a comic, until he had become the centre of attention, oblivious of the stares, the child's cries, his body now probably wet with sweat. When he finally saw me emerge from the phone booth, it was too late.

'You told them!' I heard him scream. 'You told them about Cheever!'

I nodded and pushed past him as he was seized by the child's father (tall man, grey suit, Rembrandt nose) pointing to the child screaming face down on the floor. In the din of the gawping and the commotion, I turned, turned back to the focal point of the uproar and said quietly in Burbank's ear:

'You said you were just a runner, Walter. Then run. Run. You forgot, unlike Monopoly, we're playing this game for keeps.'

Then, casually, after helping the child up (Sarah Jane), I walked away from the scrummage near the phone booth, stopping only to buy *The Times* at a near-by news-stand. I was taking the first taxi back to London, and I wanted the crossword to while away the time. With luck, and if there aren't too many anagrams, I might even finish it.

3. A Quiet Dinner for Thirteen

Though I had a short, undistinguished and totally mediocre career as an officer, I was never a gentleman, am not and never will be. I say this not out of pride or bitterness, but simply because that is the way I am, and, despite occasional and utterly foolish essays into what used to be termed Grand Society, I remain completely without any distinguishing marks of character of any kind. A girl I once knew said that there was nothing rare about me. Nothing at all. That even in my veins there ran only blood ordinaire. And she was right. The bitch.

I am in no way artistic (Van Gogh's 'Sunflowers' were eclipsed by my apathy years ago), and I can play neither cello, mouth-organ nor harp, though I was once tempted to shoot the pianist during what sounded to me like a memorial service for 'These Foolish Things'. At times, I aspire to cultural heights, attempt to learn Beethoven's symphonies by numbers, but I fail miserably, deceiving everyone but myself, like the man who carved Byron's name on the Acropolis. I merely *touch* Art. I am, however, at times capable of drawing the silhouette of a cat, have been known to linger before any painting in which flesh pink is used liberally and consequently have not only heard of Modigliani, but can also pronounce his name correctly. Para-doxically, I can understand Magritte (that visual Nabokov) but no one else; a fact that seems to impress everybody except my-self, especially when the candles are low and the port is steadily orbiting the Brie.

I do, however, read – not mainly out of choice but of neces-sity, since because of my profession I am obliged to spend hours alone in hotel rooms, train waiting-rooms, foyers. My literary tastes are catholic, though I have come to the conclusion that most writers need their poetic licences renewed; my apprecia-tion of verse is dictated by a *frisson* or a tear and nothing else;

while my ability to consume books borders on the obscene. If asked, I would place Vivian Darkbloom, Shishkov, Vladimir Sirin and Roman De La Chryn at the top of my exercise book, probably, if there is room on the same page as the biography of that notorious poet and member of the House of Lords, who was handsome to look at, but for an inconvenient limp, and was forced to leave England because of a scandal involving an incestuous affair with his sister. Abandoning his native soil, he travelled across Europe to Italy, where he set up house with a Contessa. Finally, tiring of these and a series of other affairs, he decided to redeem himself and fight for Greek liberty. Consequently, he travelled in his thirty-sixth year to Missolonghi where he died after being hit by a tram while crossing the road to buy some socks and a water-pistol for his nephew.

I myself find that a farcical story, though on reading it now (it is written in her handwriting, the letters fine, delicate, frail enough to be blown away by the slightest breeze) I feel nothing.

I have returned, not to the hotel, but to the house (she is still not there) and am sitting, staring at the books on her shelf. In Argyll, someone is no doubt scanning the platform for my arrival, and in an hour the phone here will ring. I will answer it and tell the caller that I am about to go out to dinner, given by a celebrated hostess whose card has been irritating the mirror for a week. The caller will ask no question, for in my profession I am respected enough to be given two days to act. It is a small concession, rather like a no-claim bonus in an insurance policy; for good behaviour, I am allowed forty-eight hours' meditation (in the summer I go fishing, hamper and stool) and no more. Today is Friday, which means I must make my first move towards Feather by Sunday. Since I have every intention of doing no such thing, by Monday I will probably be dead. Before that, however, I am going to take a long bath in horse-chestnut essence and open a bottle of Glenlivet.

Small luxuries such as these are, after all, the stuff of life.

*

A long ridge, flat, bleak, under an oyster Wiltshire sky (Devizes to our left), another ridge farther south separated by a valley of low hedges, abandoned ditches and the number of trees one could count on a fork. The prevailing atmosphere is bleak, devoid of life, except for the solitary silhouette of a car, parked, doors open, above us on the skyline, two miles away, waiting for our arrival. Next to me, Celandine drives slowly, her face as white as copy-paper, driving the Land-Rover he had left for us at the station and which, in the past mile, has taken on the effervescent charm of a tumbril.

No words have been spoken for fifteen minutes (the Plimsoll-line of conversation is ominously low in a situation like this), and we both merely stare fixedly at the car parked above and what it contains. It is ten days exactly since that encounter in Bath and my actions now are nothing less than certifiable. Silence, a wind cutting hard across the plateau from the north, the Land-Rover lurching momentarily across a pot-hole, pushing our two corpses against each other for a brief second, then, self-consciously, we separate.

'He wants to meet you,' she had told me two nights before (phone off the hook, her friends abandoning Denise Robins for us, C. wearing the same dress five days in a row, too frightened to return home). 'You've got to talk to him.'

'Why? I've seen him before.'

'You must see him, darling. Please.'

'But he's agreed, hasn't he?'

'Yes ... but ... I've got to be sure. Do you understand that?'

'Sure of what?'

'Sure of myself.'

'I think I'm going to throw up. I refuse to continue a conversation as trite as this. There must be something in Tolstoy we can use. Like the Bible, a phrase for every aberration.'

'You've got to see him.'

'Don't fool yourself. I don't need to see him at all. *You* have to, don't you? All the rest is mere ... camouflage.'

The hovering of a hawk draws my eye, hovering twenty, perhaps thirty feet in the air, low, before dropping to the ground, rising and flying away out of my line of vision, its claws empty. This part of England seems as fertile as the moon and produces in me the same feeling of weightlessness. A ridge, a grey sky, three trees and that car just over a mile away. The colour, I notice now, is green. Green as a privet. It must also be added that it is Celandine's car, while we are in *his* Land-Rover. The exchange therefore is not only over a wife, but also over a vehicle

Holding me close, she bursts into tears, hiding her head. I feel my body evaporate, diminishing.

The ascent now is so steep that the Land-Rover struggles even in first gear. The car is to our right now, in profile. A green Austin Mini. From the open front door protrude a pair of legs, angled down, the owner out of sight, stretched across the front seats. Two empty bottles of brown ale lie beneath the left shoe, neck to neck, while a bag of weekend groceries leans against a wheel, insignificant perhaps except for a child's drawing, fluttering against the tyre, pinned viciously to the carrier.

We park the Land-Rover twenty yards away, the engine is switched off and neither of us moves, gazing a hundred miles apart from each other at the legs, the bottles, the drawing and the horizontal figure of her husband. Silence, once more, except for the wind across the valley below, with the sky now enveloping us. I feel like a child in the darkness, for it has finally become as sentimental as that. One hundred years ago, a duel probably would be taking place (seconds clustered by tall pines, ankles in mist, jackets folded neatly on dawn grass), but today, here, just a couple of cars and the realization that she is still not yet mine. One of us is going to leave this absurd farce and I pray it isn't me. After all, I have no longer the energy for walking.

They are now both sitting in the green Austin, husband and wife, side by side, talking without looking at each other, doors closed, while I, seducer, breaker of marriages, fancy-man, stroll along the ridge, waiting self-consciously. Two walkers appear along a bridle path, dog at heel, and wave cheerily to me, then pass on. It begins to grow colder and lights appear in the distance. I have run out of cigarettes, hunger cleaves my stomach and I glance across at the car. They have been there an hour, and I, helpless, watch as she wipes her eyes. Fifteen minutes, half an hour, and I am now standing above them, the two vehicles below. For a brief while I had forgotten the reason I was there, and study the scene below, a casual observer out for a promenade, merely passing the time.

I feel like a Peeping Tom, dry-run the phrase in my mind to encourage a collage of associations of her, naked (not on a white horse. At least, not yet), but quiet, still, nervous, on my bed, awake, my face so close to hers that I can see the brushwork. More tears (the days seemed to have been filled with tears, drowning us like Alice). Phrases, the first realization of loving her saddening me to distraction; of her undressing before me shyly, and revealing herself with surprise, as if she had never been naked before, not realizing there was another texture beneath the petticoat. Other things, scattered at random – the sky is now dark. I have been waiting two hours – eager realizations of mutual heroes (Chatterton, Ravel, Bierce), books, films, trees, anecdotes, rectangles of tapestry. Contrasts, too : her belief in God, my wretched agnosticism; her status (frail aristocratic) against my lace-curtained upbringing. Politics, jokes, sex, the sweet old et cetera.

I am now totally without pain, as much a part of the ridge and the valley as the trees and the hedgerows. If a painter had canvassed the landscape, I would be in it, in detail. The cars too. A deadness . . .

Suddenly, I realize the enormity of it all, my mind resolves, confronted with the truth before me, as obvious as a brick wall and just, totally, as simple. It is as immediate as that. *I* am the one who has to leave alone, get out, get back to the crowds, huddle, as my profession demands it, in the darkness of isolation. I must abandon her now, before it is too late; before she realizes not only what my career is, but worse, much worse – that I don't love her at all. Not an ounce.

And so I begin to run, down along the ridge, stumbling, towards the road, attempting to detour the cars but he is already before me, seizing my arm and pulling me round, his face crumpling, and saying in my ear, 'You can have her then. You can have her. She'll leave you too one day, but you can have the cow. Fuck you both. Fuck you both! *Fuck* you!' and then, swaying, almost collapsing and hurrying into the Land-Rover without looking back, driving off, doors still open, and I am left alone, except for a green Austin Mini parked twenty yards before me, within which sits a strange girl, thin, fair-haired, utterly lost, and as familiar to me as a translucent Dodo.

*

The house has now taken on the dimensions of the Colosseum and I feel lost and totally redundant. I am, I repeat, superfluous. Everything about me, from the double bed to the twin closets, seems to be designed for two people, and yet only I remain, clutching a rag-bag of feed-lines, like one half of a tired music-hall act whose partner, selfishly, has died. She has left me everything, and consequently nothing. Left me sitting on my end of the see-saw, immobile, waiting pathetically for her to return, and I know, whatever the precedents, that she never will. Perhaps she never existed after all. Perhaps that bathrobe and those earrings are mine, exposing me suddenly to you as a pitiful transvestite in order to add piquancy to the story. But like it or not, there are no such exotic deviations in my character – at least not any I am prepared to confess – and the earrings have adorned only her ears, the bathrobe, her body.

*

Emerging from the water, she stands, her skin wet, calamine pink, upon the bathroom scales, staring down at the dial between her feet. Through the open door, I study her naked back, perched inelegantly on the rectangle of the machine, reminding me of a nude Andromeda I had seen in a garden in Kent that seemed to be about to topple off its pedestal through overweight, as if, behind the sculptor's back, it had over-eaten. Celandine was not yet overweight (at least not to me), apart from a slight lowering of the breasts and the pound of flesh, given to her in barter by me, which she now carried as a memento around her navel.

'Scales bloody broken again,' I hear her shout, and then she wraps the bathrobe around her, leaving only eyes and nose visible above collar and beneath pink plastic bath-hat. This triangle of skin remains the only portion of her exposed as she makes up her eyes, grotesquely, in my shaving mirror, until, finally, on turning to me, she resembles a vamp in purdah. Slowly, my hand reaches for the cord of the robe, and as it begins to fall away, I hear her say, her voice anaesthetized, 'Dominic would have been eight tomorrow, Jay. We were going to go to Greenwich to see the uniforms.'

I move away and return to a car kit I have been constructing, leaving her alone behind the closed door. In time, when she is ready, she will emerge dressed, pick up a book and read, curled up on the sofa in the next room. She may not appear for an hour or even longer, but when she does she will be ready. She may not speak, but she will be ready.

*

I am now attempting to knot the bow-tie for the third time. The expected call from Argyll arrived at 7.20 exactly. I was curt but polite and hung up, informing the caller that I was already late in my preparations to attend a dinner tonight that hinted at being boring and fashionable. However, the card had been addressed to 'Mr and Mrs Jay Mallory', and I felt one of us ought to represent the household, just in case the other one had the same thought in mind. The caller (north Welsh, I would hazard, by his accent) seemed bad-tempered at my procrastination over Feather but could, naturally, do nothing for forty-eight hours. He did however inquire about Celandine, which puzzled me, since family gossip is rarely a trait of the profession.

I attempt the bow-tie again, consider cheating with a clip-on fabrication that gives me the appearance of a pre-war bandleader, then resolve to pursue my initial efforts. I am not, as you will have perceived, a social lion by nature, but then in moments like these a man will do anything. Another hour in this terraced mausoleum and I fear I will go mad.

While completing my toiletry, I feel it fair to lay some of my cards on the table, though I reserve the right to keep the ace till later. First and foremost, I do not belong in any way (nor, like Burbank, aspire to) to that quaint club one has read so much about that has its head office in Palermo and its branches in almost every morgue north of Tampa, Florida. Despite the Machiavellian flavour of my profession, I do not care to be dictated to by a *capo-don*, or even a mastodon, advised by a *consiglieri*, or to be told to collect the pizzas from the local delicatessen by anyone who scrawls *capo-regine* on his calling card. I will eat *linguini* and drink Valpolicella with the best of you, consider Italy to be one of the most beautiful countries in Europe and have a collection of Sinatra albums that rivals Reprise Records. However, if a line must be drawn, and I suppose it must as I am still fifteen minutes too early for the soirée, I will attempt to offer at least three reasons why not a single dime of the 8,000,000,000 dollars a year profit in organized American crime (according to the U.S. Senate) ever enters my own small pocket.

Firstly, being an individualist, I refuse to be a member of any organization, neither Diners Club, golf club nor wolf pack, and though I am sure clubs promote security among those of us who are insecure, I myself prefer to be insecure alone, without fees, circulars or monthly bulletins, and certainly would hesitate in joining a club in which the chances of receiving the annual newsletter regularly were precarious, to say the least.

The second reason is less frivolous and much more fundamental. In my profession (now reaching, pensionless, its twelfth year), I have travelled extensively and met, through contacts and during my assignments, many lay brothers of the Palermo Order, including Calcedonio di Firenze, Luigi Pescara, Franco Ventotene and Cesare Alighieri. Two of these men are dead, and nothing more shall be said about that. What I *will* say, however, is that all the men I have met are distinguishable by one unique or peculiar trait – they are none of them either unique or peculiar. In America, for the Cosy Affair, the days of Lucky Luciano, pointed shoes and shoulder-holsters are as remote as the Crossing of the Red Sea, and the gorilla in your neighbourhood who drives the biggest car, lives in the gaudiest house and throws the wildest parties is probably either an upholsterer or Fu Manchu. One thing he is certainly not, is a *capo*, for that man is probably driving his kids to school, buying real-estate or going to church on Sunday. He and his *consiglieri* live in the suburbs, invest in children's playgrounds and funeral parlours, play bridge with their wives and spend their time, in America, anywhere between Lido Beach on Long Island and Grosse Pointe, Michigan. They are, in short (at least on the surface), respectable, middle-class bores, with one swimming pool, two cars, and are as conspicuous in their neighbourhood as a kerbstone.

When a barbecue in Apalachin, New York, was raided on 14 November, 1957, fifty-seven men, including a bandleader, a cheese-seller, a hearse salesman, a grocery clerk and, no doubt, a candlestick-maker, dropped their steaks as if they were as hot as their bank statements, and took to the hills. Only the host (mouth open, charcoal burning the flower-bed) was unaware that all fifty-seven varieties were members of a club that peddles, besides gruyère and *Melancholy Baby*, narcotics, prostitution, gambling and murder. 'They were all so ... so ordinary,' he protested. 'One of them even sold prayer books.' At thirty-nine years of age, I, for one, am too old to take orders from someone who only sells prayer books. Besides – which brings me to the third reason – neither Don Vitone, Don Ancona nor any other *capo* of the club has ever asked me. Not *once*. I suppose the answer is, I'm just not respectable or religious enough for them. Especially now, on a cold winter evening like this, with my marriage collapsing around me like Gomorrah.

And so I work alone (and lately, live alone too), freelance, under-paid, affiliated to an organization that is as small and dependable as the family butcher. I am still in work and alive (today, I repeat, being Friday) because I am reliable and cautious. I have also, by some freak mixture of genes, developed a remarkable talent for remembering details. If we were in the parlour now and you placed twenty-six objects on a tray before me for a mere second, I could not only recount each one of them, I could also throw in as a bonus the colour, order and arrangement, plus an uncanny description of the tray itself.

My mind is appendixed hourly by lists of facts, ranging from geraniums (double and semi-double *Zonal pelargoniums*) to Norse gods. I can out-Roget Roget, quote verbatim any stanza I have read twice, so that my memory is now sprocketed like a reel of film, infinite, ever-unwinding and utterly useless. Show me a man's study and I will tell you not only exactly how he lives, but, more specifically, how he ought to die. Death is natural. Consequently murder must never seem *un*natural, if it is to succeed with impunity. It must appear to be an inevitable conclusion to the man's life, not a premature aberration. For example, an assassin who pushes a subject suffering from vertigo off the Eiffel Tower will be in jail before his victim hits the ground, not because a man suffering from vertigo might not quite easily fall from the Eiffel Tower, but because he would never be up there in the first place. A puerile statement, you may well say, but many murderers have hung for naivety as banal as that. I myself am still alive, undetected, my secrets (except for the occasional orgasms of flamboyance) intact. When I myself am hanged, and it may well be, like the washing, on Monday, mum – God rest her soul – will still be the word.

I have become, you now understand, like a computer, making me such a fine professional, as well as (I see now all too well) such a pathetically wretched husband.

*

Friday. 8.15 p.m. It is time to depart for my candle-lit dinner. I am looking presentable and yet slightly eccentric (lace-ruffled shirt, velvet waistcoat), as is required and as befits (to the un-initiated) the parasitical husband of an heiress. No doubt the news of Celandine's exit has already reached the actors waiting in the wings, but my face is framed for poker, my temperature steady and my blood happily revitalized by the malt whisky. I will turn up alone, be enigmatic, avoid gossip and sidelong glances, and mention Celandine's name not once. If someone else does, I will ignore it. If she herself does, I will, of course, being a man of ice, run hysterically out of the room.

Her comb, I notice, still lies on the carpet by the door. I step over it as if it were the width of the Nile, then leave. As I am about to close the door, a message drops from the letter-box where it must have been hurriedly placed by someone who did not care to be seen. In my car, I open it, after switching on the engine. It reads: 'Start plucking the Feather before Sunday is out.' That is all. I assume therefore that it is either a biblical tract or some obscure and rather pointless proverb, and so, naturally, tear it up and throw it out of the window and drive away.

When I arrived, the strip of roadway before the terraced Georgian house resembled nothing less than a chauffeurs' convention, as the uniformed drivers loitered against limousines and sports cars like arrogant street arabs. It was going to be, I could see, one of those exclusive evenings where the guests talk with the corners of their eyes, discuss banalities with the gravity of Galileo and then leave early with their mistresses, or late with their wives. It would not, in any way, be like the Apalachin barbecue, but before entering the door I knew I would meet as infinite a variety of guests, living illustrations from all the best books in town – *Burke's Peerage*, *Baily's Hunting Directory*, *Who's Who*, *The British Film Year Book* and no doubt, in this sweet year of grace, *Black Beauty*. For a moment, I felt like accelerating straight on round the square and back to the Glenlivet, but curiosity (and hope) restrained me. I therefore parked impertinently before someone's Rolls, cut the chauffeur dead and approached the house.

The door was opened, naturally, by a butler with the face of an out-of-work embalmer, who measured my status briefly with his eyes, then reluctantly allowed me to enter. I was then abandoned in the hallway for two full minutes (chatter to the left behind a mahogany door, a wall of prints, somebody emerging from a toilet, seeing me, then hurrying away) before the hostess herself finally arrived, taking my hand and easing my irritation with a smile one could auction at Sotheby's.

I had met her before, of course, and had heard all the scandals while hiding behind the arras, but still retained the infinite ability to be impressed by her. I had listened as she was described by her relatives as a coquette and a du Barry, by her ex-lovers (landscape gardeners and that garage-hand from Perth) as a whore and by her enemies as an evergreen social-climber. As a hostess she was no doubt superb, being not only beautiful but totally unimaginative, so that, conscious of both qualities, she visually seduced each guest while parroting the requisite flatteries in a breathless voice she had retained, like her school satchel, since she was fourteen years of age.

She was still beautiful – encouraging sniggers in the parlour and a list of anecdotes as long as a poplar, but as I stood in the hallway, gazing politely into that face seemingly painted with colours from her daughter's water-colour tin, I myself, without embarrassment, was enchanted. Circe she may be to the social leeches who gobbled her food, rapier concealed, but to me, romantic paradox that I am, she was the most refreshing creation in an urban clique that boasted neither taste nor good manners. Mrs Harriette Greville had both, and if I had a golden apple, I would give it to her and to hell with Aphrodite.

If anyone mentioned Celandine this evening, it wouldn't be her, and even though the food she served was invariably inedible, the table would not suffer because of *her* presence. 'She's a selfish, vain and predatory cow, and her husband is a cuckold,' some turtle-necked bore had once whispered to me as he edged towards her on the sofa to tell her of his latest coup. 'It's revolutionary,' he shouted in her ear. I remember she turned, and smiled and nodded, giving the speaker the attention most people reserve only for God or for themselves. A remarkable woman, Mrs Harriette Greville. Remarkable and utterly, painfully, fragile.

'I'm so glad you came on your own, Jay,' she said as I released her hand. 'You're the only person I really wanted to be here, and you are. Besides, I must confess there's one extra female, which settles everything. Don't you think that's a marvellous face? Ford Madox Brown. Dark and gloomy like a pirate's attic. Do come and meet the others – they haven't said a word all evening. One's a film producer, I think. Hungarian of course. Oh, and Hugh Praed is here. You must have known him at Oxford.'

'Only vaguely. He was always on the river, while I stayed on dry land.'

'So did I. Much more fun. Reading Waugh. I remember when – no, I won't say that or I'll start giving clues to my age. We'd better get into the arena before all is revealed. Take my arm, Jay. Take it now and return to it hourly. I'm going to get drunk and so are you. I'm going to get drunk and idolize the ugliest man in the room. That's how I feel right now. I wish you were ugly, Jay, then I could idolize you, but I do so hate unrequited love. Don't you?'

*

> 'She is only a child, blond, laughing . . . and sad
> She does not smile and she never cries;
> But deep in her eyes, when she lets you drink there,
> Trembles a gentle silver lily, the poet's flower.

'God, Jay – isn't that fantastic? Look at his face. Blaise Cendrars. Isn't it just *too* fantastic? Listen.

> 'For she is my love and the other women
> Have only dresses of gold on tall bodies of flame,
> My poor friend is so lonely,
> She is quite naked, has no body – she is too poor.

'Too poor, Jay. Too poor. Not like us. Not, alas, like us.'

*

There were thirteen people who sat down later for dinner, which seemed ominous to say the least, though Easter, fortunately, was four months away. We sat in a circle, but I won't bore you with details, except to say that the guest-list included a publisher whose claim towards his contribution to his writers' success was as immodest as a fig-leaf, and two politicians from opposing parties, who agreed about everything except the wine and whose views terrified one to the marrow. Between them sat an actress of little repute (she once played Mother Inferior) who had apparently appeared naked in all her films, as well as in five advertisements, three magazines and between the sheets of half of the subscribers to Hansard. She was, in short, a poor cliché, and will consequently not be referred to again. Others: a Shelleyan son of a baronet who rolled his own brand of cigarettes and smoked them only in the garden, in private, or in the toilet; then beyond the candelabra (I am now concentrating on the veal) those twin pillars of society, Robin and Annabel, who would allow no one to come between them, least of all Samson. Mrs Harriette Greville to my left, then myself, eyes down, hating it all. If God is alive and everywhere, let us all hope He doesn't have to sit through this awful dinner.

Celandine, of course, is not here. I am not yet so immune that I reserve her appearance till last – and so I am obliged to avert my gaze, up-ending the decanter, until, halfway between the main course and the dessert, I become conscious of the woman on my right whom I have apparently ignored all evening. She is speaking:

'Did you hear the news?'

'Pardon?'

She is about twenty-five, blonde, with a pretty face that is not quite right, as if it has once been dropped and been hurriedly pieced together before the light failed. The nose and mouth are familiar, though I have never seen them before except on a portrait hanging over a marble mantel in Lausanne. The subject of the painting (a Swiss matron with a neck that could have supported the Acropolis) died in 1783, while my neighbour is very much alive, totally attractive, and has that air of reassurance one finds only in professional pianists, borzois and knole-sofas. Grey eyes, long straight nose, Cordelia's breasts, the dimpled mouth of a figurine.

'The news,' she repeated. 'Another murder.'

'Oh?' I replied casually, declining the soufflé and acknowledging a smile from the hostess. Neighbour on right must be the extra female. Extra *married* female, too, I notice, as I glance at a ring on her finger that could save my life.

'At London Airport. It was on the news. A man was knifed to death in the departure lounge.'

'Our export regulations are very strict,' I replied, not looking at her. 'Who was he? Anyone famous?'

'Not to me. George –'

She has now turned towards a man across the table who I know is not her husband, since George Holroyd and I are old friends. When George is bored, he invites me to his house in Hertfordshire, and when *I* am bored, I go. We both spend the weekend alternately playing Chinese chequers, drinking whisky and admiring his farm. Last year, his wife left him for a boy of nineteen, taking one of his cars and driving to St Mawes. He showed me a card she sent him a week later. It was quite a pretty little thing depicting a small smugglers' cove with one or two boats drawn up on the rocks and the distant figure of a man sitting on a bench, obviously unaware that his image was destined to be sent to all corners of the world accompanied, like the Queen, by a fourpenny stamp. On the back of this particular card were the words: 'George. Sorry but this is the only way. I love him. Keep the Daumier if you wish. A.' There is very little one can write on a postcard, but as George told me as I handed it back to him, carefully, as if it were porcelain, 'It says all, Mallory. But I'm pleased about the Daumier.'

'George,' my neighbour repeats, 'what was the name of that man who was murdered at London Airport?'

'Burbage,' George replies.

'No, not Burbage. Burbage was an actor.'

'Bur*bank*, then.'

'Yes. Burbank.'

She then turned back to me and said quietly:

'Burbank. I've never heard of him, nor have you probably, but George remembers everything.'

'So do I,' I reply.

'Do you? My name is Celia Deverell. Will you remember that?'

'Yes. Jay Mallory.'

'I know. Harriette told me.'

'What else did she tell you?'

'Nothing – except that your son was killed by a car two years ago.'

'Stepson. How do you do, Mrs Deverell.'

'How do you do, Jay.'

And that really was that. We talked for a quarter of an hour until the ladies adjourned, and I was left with the port, a cigar and a group of men who immediately indulged in the tasteless jubilance of undertakers during a plague. Ignoring them, I thought of Burbank, not with pity but with fear. The speed of his death reminded me all too vividly of my own vulnerability and my own thoughts of betrayal. I must send Mrs Burbank a newspaper clipping of his death for the scrapbook, for I was grateful, at least, that his end had been sudden. If he had talked, I might as well be in Macedonia.

After half an hour, the two sexes met again in the drawing-room, and I talked for a further two hours with Mrs Celia Deverell, as we sat side by side on two Chippendale chairs near the window. Regarding the conversation, not a syllable can be repeated since in all that time she revealed nothing of herself, allowing me only occasional glimpses of her, well-rehearsed but incomplete, like Salome winding up her act after the fifth veil in order to leave her audience tantalized and utterly unfulfilled. Oh, anecdotes were exchanged. A joke or two, and once I almost fell into the pit myself (*Celia* is too dangerously close to *Celandine*. The modern tongue adjusts far too slowly). Once I was on the point of telling her about my wife – a gesture of hers reminded me too painfully of one I thought I had forgotten – but controlled, reluctantly, the desire.

Across the room, I could see Harriette sitting as sober as Knox, watching us like a mother-hen, and at one point joining us to discuss something absurd like cricket or the latest stage-play, then moving away, pedestal under one arm, which an actor had apparently mislaid while the attention was focused on someone else. Then, as if by telepathy, Celia Deverell talked about marriage – but George's, not mine.

'It was his own fault,' she said. 'He gave her too much.'

'Too much? I thought women complained they received too little.'

'Of course, Jay, but too little is better than too much. Treat a woman as if she is the most precious thing on earth and she will leave you, like Angela left George. Treat her, however, as if she were the second most precious thing and she will stay – if only in order to scratch out the eyes of her superior. In love, as in bridge, the man who puts all his cards on the table has no longer any control over the game.'

'I'll bear that in mind,' I replied.

'Please do.'

Someone then suggested a game for the intellectuals, who were distinguishable by being either drunker or more loud-voiced than the rest. We all had to guess quotations, read out earnestly by a girl in a sequinned dress, who spoke with one arm constantly up in the air. She reminded me of that juggler's assistant, invariably called Babs, who appears in the background to the act, does nothing but pick up the Indian clubs, then bows at the finale. Babs read twenty quotations and I, not being in the mood, guessed only one. Listen, and I'll tell you the answer later:

> The sand and sea have had their way,
> And moons of spring and autumn –
> All, save I,
> And even my vision will be erased
> As a cameo the waves claim again.

If you have guessed right, you would probably have liked my wife, for it is, of course (the knife turns) by Hart Crane.

*

'Jay? ... Jay, where have you been? Jay, can you hear me? I've been trying to phone you for hours. Jay – guess what? The divorce has come through. McClure has just told me. Jay – don't you understand? We can now get married. The divorce has finally come through ... Oh, Jay, I love you. I love you so much. So very ... *very* much.'

*

For a brief moment, it seems as if Celia's fur coat has been stolen. She remembered leaving it in the hall, but now it has gone. After a flurry of panic (butler's head disappearing behind the screen, cry from upstairs) it is found in the bathroom.

'Well, good night.'

She turns to me, walks to the door, then hesitates:

'By the way, are you doing anything this weekend?'

'This weekend?' I ask, my mind cancelling out lists of excuses. 'Not really ...'

'Well, look ... we're having a few guests at our house for the weekend and perhaps you'd like to join us. It's right on the other side of the world but you could drive or take a train.'

There was a momentary delay, then Celia, on cue, took my arm.

'Please come. It might be fun.'

'All right,' I reply. 'Where is it?'

'Boronsay.'

'Boronsay? Where the hell is that?'

'Oh dear, no one ever knows. Look it up in the *A.A.* There's my number. Come any time tomorrow and stay as long as you like. I love unexpected guests. Good night, Jay.'

Then she is gone and I am left alone with Harriette, turning aside to stifle a yawn, her mouth large enough to contain a tennis-ball. Turning back, cheeks flushed (husband snoring, no school for kiddy tomorrow), she mentions casually that I am the last guest. There is no one else but she and I, and Annabel's is still open. But by now, dear Mrs Greville, at three o'clock in the morning, you look your age, and in the real dark night of the soul it is either small-bummed girls or sleep for me. So I bid her good night, taking her hand, then pull my hand away and enter the cold, effervescent night air. The street below is deserted except for my car and the tail-light of a Rolls as it departs, carrying Mrs Celia Deverell to her Arcadia.

When I return home, I hear the telephone – I must ask the engineers for a different colour, beige rings far too much – and answer it wearily. Same voice. North Welsh.

'Well?' the voice asks. 'Why are you still in London?'

'If I wasn't, how could I answer your call? Anyway, I'm going away for the weekend. To Boronsay.'

'Boronsay? Where's that?'

'Do what I have just done. Look it up in the *A.A.* You'll be surprised.'

I mentally see him reaching for his guide-book, but I know that he will not be surprised at all when he finds it. For ironically, like a poor joke, I have been invited by a complete stranger to spend a few days in the very place I have made every effort to avoid. I have been invited by the enigmatic Mrs Celia Deverell to Argyll.

I will, of course, accept the invitation, brushing aside all my sixth-form thoughts of a sinister coincidence. After all, I've never seen Argyll before, least of all Boronsay, and it's about time Jay Mallory, during this weekend of all weekends, took a holiday.

4. Gatsby, Ophelia and One Other

I am not a man who normally wakes up in bad humour, but the next morning – and I make no apologies – I quarrelled unashamedly with the paper-boy.

*

The girl is fifteen and nude and walks along the tide away from me, oblivious of me, walking away from me along the tidewash, gazing at a brooch she carries in her hand. I stand in the sea, my trousers rolled up, held up by braces, a pipe in my mouth (bowler on head), and watch her pass, apathetic to the trombone burning in the cerulean sky, watch her thin nude body walk past, for she belongs to another canvas, has walked along the surf-wash of mine and is no longer there. Her own canvas is now uninhabited, but a third, no doubt hanging in a private collection, is annexed by her. René writes his name as I paddle. I will move no more for he has written his name, sealing my movements for ever in oil and varnish. Later I dream of Durkin, but only for a brief moment for I am unable to sleep, and so dress while still in darkness. It is probably better this way, because it is not my body, regrettably, that needs rest, it is my whole life.

*

It is not, of course, the fault of the paper-boy, for, like everyone else, he has his orders to pursue, but I do object to inefficiency, especially at seven o'clock in the morning. I had been sitting in the kitchen, drinking coffee, thinking of Feather, planning my next move. In this profession, as is to be expected, one is kept in total ignorance not only of one's hierarchy (if any), but also, more importantly, of the instigator of the assignment. Whoever was putting up the money to eliminate someone he or she no longer cared for was usually none of my business. Since it is a clandestine arrangement and not a television panel-game I am not paid to ask questions, and to tell you the truth I normally could not care less who my client is. I merely play my pipe to the required tune as skilfully as I can, collect my reward and move on. Feather, however, was something else, and the questions that ricocheted around my brain at that god-forsaken hour were far from being mere curiosity. Who (or what) was Feather, who wanted him dead and why (the coffee I make is pitiful) should the bait of eight thousand pounds (two thousand going to the agent) be so deliberately irresistible? At this point in the weekend, I could answer none of these enigmas, especially now that Walter Burbank was dead, the toast was burning and my mind was distracted by the arrival, at last, of the paper-boy.

I had seen him approach the house from the kitchen window, and consequently, eager to read about the details of Burbank's exit (in the departure lounge, no less), I hurried to the front door to collect the newspapers personally. We exchanged brief good-mornings, then as he was turning away (one hand already searching for the neighbour's *Tatler*), I called him back:

'You've made a mistake,' I said, handing back to the youth one of the newspapers. 'This one doesn't belong to us.'

I was presented with a frown of petulant irritation, then the newspaper concerned was studied and returned.

'No mistake, sir,' (politeness at this hour? The boy will go far). 'It should have arrived yesterday but we had to have it sent.'

I looked at the newspaper again, limbering up for a verbal bout. It was cold, dark and I was in a bad mood, but I still had never heard of a paper called, if you can believe it, the *Oban Times*.

'Listen,' I said, my voice tuning into the right balance of indignation and authority. I may not pay the bills but I do have my self-respect. 'Listen, I have never heard of the *Oban Times*, nor am I passionate to learn about it now. I have never read it and do not intend to begin at my age. If it's some kind of religious call to arms, drop it in the vicar's font and not on my front door-step. Now, take it back.'

The youth didn't move, and I could see by the look in his eyes that it was now going to be a battle of the generations.

'The *Oban Times*, sir,' he began with that voice of polite insolence usually brandished by commissionaires, hotel barmen and town councillors, 'is *not* a religious paper and never has been. It was, in fact, specifically ordered two days ago from this house, and I can vouch for that because it was me who answered the phone.'

'Oh really?' I replied, smarting from that word 'vouch' and staring him straight in the eye. 'You answered the phone did you? And from whom, may I ask – or is it too much trouble?'

'From Mrs Mallory, sir. From your wife.'

I recall reading in a book once, or perhaps I was told on a train to Newcastle, that at certain moments of quietude, when the body and the mind are completely passive, one can feel the earth revolve under one. This, as it happened, was not one of those moments, though I accept the conjecture, because I could feel nothing, nothing whatsoever. I could merely gawp like an idiot at a fifteen-year-old youth standing two steps below me and wonder why Celandine, walking out of our house and my life for ever, would take it into her head to order a newspaper I had never heard of, called, of all things, the *Oban Times*. My repartee is now staggering.

'Wait a minute. You said you had to have the paper sent. Sent from where?'

'From where it says. It's a local paper, you see.'

'Local paper for what?'

'If you read it, sir, you'll find out. It's the local paper for Argyll.'

This time the world revolved. There is no doubt about that now. And, regarding that fact, on this particular Saturday morning, standing immobile on a cold, wet pavement in west London, I could, in two seconds flat, have convinced a camel. Someone, somewhere, has just re-tied the Gordian knot.

*

'Cel-andine. That's C-e-l, not ... Actually, it's really Celandine-Dora, but that's too much of a mouthful for anyone, even for someone with a mouth like mine. So Celandine. Named after a great-aunt. When you visit my parents' house, you'll see her portrait on the stairs. Daddy adored her, and secretly I think he had a slight affair with her. Anyway, she remains on the stairs, looking down at the visitors like an Olympian goddess. Pale and pink with the colour of a Regency library. Do you know what I mean? That warm brown. I never met her, because she died before I was born. One of the gardeners found her entangled in the weeds of an ornamental pond. Nobody ever knew why. Anyway, that's where I got my name. I used to hate it once. At school, I used to be called Salt-Cellar for some extraordinary reason.'

'Perhaps because boys made passes at you.'

'Oh, Jay ... do be serious. Anyway, it's an awful joke, and besides, it was an all-girls' school. I like *your* name though. Is it Jay like Jay, or J initial?'

'Just Jay. Christened after no one.'

'Not even after Gatsby?'

'No, I'm afraid, not even after Gatsby.'

'He ended up in a pond, too.'

'Swimming pool. And he was shot.'

'Same thing really. You see, both our names are writ on water. Well, in a way ...'

'I think we ought to go back to the party. Your husband might be looking for you.'

'Oh, I think we can risk that, don't you?'

'I still think we ought to go back to the party.'

'All right – if you promise to see me again. Another day.'

'I have a rule never to have affairs with married women.'

'Have you, Jay? How marvellous. God, what a relief. We'll just be ships passing in the night.'

'I am however going to go to the Turner collection on Tuesday. Will you come?'

'Of course. I love Turner more than almost anything in the whole world. I'll wear my yellow dress – just for him.'

*

When I phoned George half an hour later, after reading the papers, the number was engaged. I therefore dithered for a further fifteen minutes (note to the milkman, abrupt halt on *Five Down* [10, 4]) which I blamed on the paper-boy, plus a further self-pitying tour of the house, before telephoning again.

'George. Jay Mallory. Can you meet me in an hour?'

'In an *hour*? I'm still in bed.'

'All right, two hours, George. I have to talk to you.'

Silence. George is studying his watch. Outside, the first laundry van has passed by.

'Oh . . . all right. Where?'

'I thought Kenwood would be pleasant this time of the year. It opens at ten. I looked it up.'

'Looked *what* up, Mallory?'

'George – why don't you listen? You *are* on your own, aren't you?'

'Of course, I'm bloody well on my own.'

'Kenwood. Ten o'clock inside. Oh, and George – fourteen letters, ten and four, "Victorian Baby Hatchery". Begins with G. Last letter H, I think.'

'I haven't the faintest idea –'

'Think about it. I'll see you in an hour.'

I could hear the telephone at the other end rattle as its owner fumbled for the bedside table, then receiver and hook met. I then waited for two more minutes and dialled George again to discover, without too much surprise, that his number was once more engaged. It would, I knew, be engaged for a further half an hour until he shaved and dressed (invariably in dark blue) and took a slow walk, stick in hand, Fido at heel, across the heath towards our rendezvous. I myself would drive to Hampstead, having long ago given up even the slightest nod towards exercise, and was consequently granted the dubious pleasure of remaining a further twenty minutes in a house, surrounded (I hesitate to repeat it, but bear with me. We'll soon be with George) by her decorations, her books, those calls and those enthusiasms, yesterday's edition of the *Oban Times* and that damnable viaduct of spaces bisecting the crossword. For the first time since Suez, my breakfast was bottled in Scotland, though I restricted myself to five glasses. I was, after all, taking the car and one can never be too careful, especially in London, on a day like this.

When I finally arrived at Kenwood (renovated, as I learnt, via the Butes and the Mansfields, by Robert Adam) I was first welcomed by George's dog. He was tied by his lead to a railing before the north front, and greeted me, recognizing the relationship we had built up over the years, with total apathy. I could not exactly blame him, since it had begun to rain and he was eager, like me, to be free. Robert Adam was insensitive to his misery, and so, it appeared, was George, who by now was probably pacing the vestibule, checking his watch. When I joined him two minutes later, his best friend was two hundred yards away, in open land, en route for the woods.

'George Brummell is the elder child,' I said approaching George, who was now in the Old Tea Room, studying a portrait of two pink-ribboned children.

'He looks like a girl.'

'Blame it on Reynolds. Not on his father. By the way, I let Fido go.'

'I thought you might. I called him Fido, you know, because I'm called George. Common names make ... You're drunk, Jay.'

'Almost.'

During the drive north to Hampstead, I had tried to remember the first time I had met George Holroyd, but despite my arrogant facility for remembering details George, unhappily, remains in the enigmatic past, pale like Islay Mist. He was never in the Services, at least, not in mine, and yet over the years we total opposites had adopted a form of mutual attachment which so far was unshakeable. He knew more about me than I about him, but I never inquired. I had once met his wife, Angela, long before he married her, just after her first and only true lover had abandoned her for a Drury Lane chorine. Clichés abound, I realize, but that somehow is the fact of the matter. I remember that when the lover left her (his name is irrelevant) she stripped the apartment they had shared of every single object. Not only the inside, but also the outside, and it remained totally bare for six months, except, of course, for the pillowcases which she hung out every morning to dry.

George met her in The Huntsman (equestrian pursuits aroused a common *frisson*), had married her within a month, and now she too was gone, leaving him utterly unchanged on the surface, but decaying, like a neglected tooth, from within. By chance, he had acquired some money which cauterized his wounds for a while (gin, Crockford's, a table at the Mirabelle, an alien bottom sliding beneath his electric blanket), and then suddenly, that about-face of conscience that left him gasping, pitifully alone, except for Fido, and now and again someone like me. George was too young to lament and too old to begin again, and so pursued a tired war against the age by hunting and shooting in the country and by being seen, a stoop-backed aristocrat, at all the worst weekend retreats in the home counties. He was, alas, too conventional even for gossip, playing mah-jongg with only sensible skill and being always the last to be placed at table, in between nanny and youngest child. No one hated George, nor indeed did anyone love him. They merely borrowed from him, used his house (as I did) as a stop-over on the A1 to the North or, most viciously of all, made love to his wife.

Only one scandal, if that is what you want, can be presented in evidence against him, and even that is pathetically banal and would buy no one a high tea, not even in Edinburgh. The story is that he was found in the bathroom of a thirteen-year-old daughter of a Scottish peer while Eastering at their house. The girl, naked and as developed as a March daffodil, had, through embarrassment, allowed him to linger over his excuses that he had lost his way, but had screamed (narcissistic echo, hands zig-zagging across a body that had not yet decided on its cynosure) as he attempted to remove the chair separating observer from slide. The escapade had not been forgotten, especially as that young convent girl was the same Angela who later became his wife. By then, her breasts had cleverly marked time with the remainder of her figure to enhance not only her own entrance into the salon, but the salon itself.

We are now, by the way, having moved on through the winter beauty of the house (Boudoir, Orangery, Lobby), in the Music Room, neither of us having said a word, toneless before a rather mediocre Rembrandt.

'I have to talk to you,' I said, my voice low though we are the only visitors. 'I want your advice.'

'Talk here.'

'No. Outside. I want to ask you what you know about a man called Feather.'

For a moment, George hesitated, his mind ringing changes of thought, then, non-committal, touched my arm and said:

'Gooseberry bush.'

'Pardon?'

'Gooseberry bush. "Victorian Baby Hatchery"? Fourteen letters beginning with G. Gooseberry bush.'

A smile, then:

'All right, Mallory. Let's go outside and see if we can find Fido.'

'I've never heard of him. Feather, you say?'

'Feather. He's a millionaire, so he couldn't be too hard to trace.'

'Never heard of him. If you ask me, he doesn't exist.'

'Six thousand pounds says he does.'

'*Feather?*'

'Fea-ther.'

The rain was constant now but pleasantly refreshing. We had emerged on to the terrace and were descending the slope towards the sham bridge the first Earl had positioned, like a child with a toy garden set, to the south-east of the landscape. Beyond, trees, lake, heath and, no doubt, Fido. Beside me, my companion had erected an umbrella as large as a marquee and was walking head down, feet placed carefully one before the other, oblivious of everything. In summer, concerts are performed on the lawns and the Adam portico is lit by searchlights, but as far as George was concerned we might as well have been in the Sahara. It was now ten forty and I was hungry and suddenly feeling totally alienated from everything. For a brief moment, I saw myself, lead-footed, walking wearily in the wake of another man, gazing at myself, at my face, as if it were in fine print. Thoughts overlap now and a monologue (not mine or Hamlet's) begins:

'You shouldn't have said Kenwood, Mallory. Not here. Not among all this. Not here. Not where Angela and I walked, up there. If you had suggested seeing the Library, I would have thrown up. We came here first when there was snow on the ground, all ... over the ground. White house, white snow, children with toboggans, it was like a Breughel painting. Angela said that. "It's like a Breughel, George." Children and nannies, figures in a white landscape ...'

Vita used to write in that tower, Jay. Don't you think it's fantastic? She did all this garden herself. The white garden, everything. Herb garden. It has to be your favourite place too. It's always been mine. Always.

'... pillars, snowdrops. Oh dear, Mallory, I thought I'd got over it by now. The two of us, like two old spinsters on a sea-front, aren't we? Lamenting. Two old spinsters on a ... But shall I tell you something, Mallory? Shall I tell you why I knew she would never come back? Never?'

Fido has appeared at last, ignoring his master and running towards me. Black Labrador, very common, but marvellous with kiddies. *Sissinghurst.*

'She took her baby-pillow. Took it, Mallory. It was the most precious thing in the world. When I saw that was gone, I then knew she had left me for ever. She'd had it as a child, you see –'

I am suddenly very still, staring directly at George, the dog irritating my feet, staring directly at him, at George, and I hear myself saying:

'Celandine didn't run away. Of course, she didn't run away. What you said ... just now. She didn't run away. You see, she left her figurine. It's a small object, utterly worthless –' I am now jabbering, one foot kicking away a Labrador, my voice rising – 'a Regency man, but it was the only thing *she* ever cared for. She took it across Europe in a box of cotton wool like an egg. She left it, George. On the mantelpiece. Don't you see? Celandine didn't run away at all.'

'Fido! Go away. Fido – do you hear what I say? That's why I tied him up, Mallory. You really shouldn't have let him loose.'

'She was taken. Celandine was ... taken away. Taken in case I turned down Feather.'

'Oh God, Mallory, you *are* dramatic. People don't –'

'George, that's why she ordered the *Oban Times*. To tell me. She was taken away to Argyll.'

The house is far above us now, delicate and deserted.

Absurdities pour out of me, but there *must* be substance in straws. There has to be. No soliloquies, merely observation. After nine years one has at least that. I stare at George as he kneels to grasp the collar of the dog, avoiding my eye, then I turn and walk away, hesitate as he catches up with me.

'Don't try and avoid it, Mallory. Women are bitches. They take everything they can, then run. Usually with the most worthless creature they can find. It's their way. I know how you feel, but believe me, you've got to face the facts.'

'Then why did she leave the figurine and no note?'

'God knows. Why do women do anything?'

'Or order the *Oban Times*? She must have done it from a phone box, a moment on her own while their back was turned, knowing I wasn't home but had to –'

'Look, Mallory, I'm going to have to get the lead for this bloody dog. I'm not chasing after him. Why the hell didn't Angela take *him* instead of her damn pillow.'

'Let him go, George.'

'Him too?'

'Let him go. I want you to tell me if you will find out about Feather for me?'

'Not here. Can you come to Hertfordshire? I'm leaving in an hour. I might be able to find out there.'

'I'll drop by on my way north.'

'Where are you going?'

'Argyll. Where else?'

For a brief moment, the Labrador was forgotten and we both watched it as it broke loose and ran back down the slope towards the lake. George's face was now almost hidden by the umbrella but I knew he was puzzled.

'Why on earth are you going to Argyll?'

'There's no other place now that I would rather go in the world. The Fates, George. Jay is going to Argyll. Everything points there. Feather, Celandine ... Besides, I have been invited by your friend last night at dinner.'

'Couldn't be Harriette. Oh, no – not Celia Deverell.'

'Who else? I'm going to accept, George. But first I want to know all you can find out about Feather. Everything.'

George didn't reply for a while, his body retreating within

the folds of the umbrella like a bat. Then suddenly, a hand appeared, palm up, hesitated, then his face appeared, peering up at me, smiling, through the rain.

'Do you mind, Mallory, but while we're here, I would love to re-visit the Library. It has the most perfect ceiling I've ever seen. Don't you think? Do be gracious and come with me. I don't think I could see it on my own. Not just yet. Not quite just yet . . .'

And then he was gone, hurrying up the slope, holding the umbrella high like a parachute, running over the wet grass towards the terrace and into the building, so that I had to run breathlessly to catch up with him, taking a short cut beside the flower-beds to meet him in the Library. But when I reached the room, he wasn't there. Nor was he likely to be for I could see him walking back in the distance across the lawn, throwing a stick for the dog, walking, umbrella now rolled up, back home across the heath.

Three hours later, after lunch (eggs, beans, apple), I was driving across London towards the road to the North. In my luggage, I had packed only one extra item besides swimming shorts, a Browning automatic and a dinner-suit – a cheap, slightly chipped porcelain figurine of a Regency gamekeeper (complete with faithful hound) wrapped rather haphazardly in cotton wool.

5 . Feathers

I am well aware that, despite the resilience of your suspension
of disbelief, I cannot say that my marriage has been a happy
one. Far from it. From the first month (it had begun that early)
our mutual realization that this legal confinement we had
chosen for ourselves was not paradise, nor ever would be, had
filled us both not only with terror but with a strange form of
overwhelming sadness that reduced Celandine to tears and myself to cold, pitiless dispassion. Our varying moods would sometimes continue for such a long time, weeks even, that a sudden
moment of unexpected happiness would strike us both with
such incredulous alarm that we would scurry away from it as if
it were the monsoon following the sun and not the reverse. In
time, of course, we both in our individual ways began to
recognize those rare pleasures – I am embarrassed to describe
them for I realize they will mean nothing to you – and would
savour them gratefully, and for a brief moment echoes of our
first meeting would unite us once more and we would move on,
not necessarily looking at each other, but at least in a parallel
direction.

Celandine, I believe, was the first to take a lover (a notorious
rake who had eased her melancholy while she was alone in
Ravenna with Dominic), which she told me about, ridiculously,
a month later, relating the details in a matter-of-fact voice as if
reading out an insignificant news item. I remember I had said
nothing whatsoever, nor showed any reaction by even the
slightest gesture. She had wanted to be scourged, stripped,
beaten to a pulp, and I had failed her by behaving like neither a
husband nor a judge, but like a stone gnome some people keep
in their gardens to protect the wisteria. From that moment on,
our own sex life became as passionate as a railway time-table,
performed (if ever) out of habit, necessary but without fore-

thought, like placing condiments together on the table in the hope that they might add spice to a meal that had long since lost its flavour. And yet, despite everything, never once did Celandine leave or even threaten that she might, and I know (the truth comes easily when I treat you as a stranger) that I often gave her not one single reason to remain by my side. For weeks I would be away on an assignment I could never discuss with her, and when I returned, my mind reduced to the frailty of a millstone, I would retire from her sight, both mentally and physically, in order to pummel myself back into some form of humanity.

In the last four years, her lovers became more numerous and more indiscreet, selected from a coat-rack of acquaintances and strangers she met at parties, previews, dinners and any other social function for which she could beg an admission. Invitations came addressed only to her, and the telephone suddenly developed a mute affliction if ever I was the one who answered it. Scandals seeped back to me through all the usual mink-lined sewers and once I even caught her naked in a child's nursery, her face white, the door to the garden open, footsteps disappearing into the darkness. 'Husband arrived, Don Juent,' I said casually, spelling out the pun, and then left, taking all her clothes, leaving the house (somewhere, if it matters, in Berkshire) and drove back to London, stopping only to drop her gown and underwear in the Thames just near Henley.

She returned the next morning in borrowed clothes and left a poem of love on my desk, written during the emotional drought of the darkness. If I could I would quote it now to show not only that she had loved me once, but that I myself love her insanely still. But I never received the poem, for on her return, I had already left to kill S. and was delayed long enough for the sonnet to enter the fire when her phone failed to ring.

Two years later, we both resolved to try once again to play our chosen roles as best we could, and were even blissfully happy for a month after a nostalgic visit to Paris, and returned to our home, hand in hand, in our seventh year of marriage, closer than we had ever been in our whole lives. I remember we approached the house like two giggling children, running up the steps to the front door to discover within a mere minute that no matter what might happen now, things could not ever be the same again and that not even a miracle could reunite us, even if we wished it. Dominic, her son, had been run over and killed by a car two hours before our arrival, while crossing the road after buying some chocolate drops and a sherbet fountain at the corner store. His present from Paris (a motorized scale-model of a Citroën DS) still rests unopened, untouched, on the lower shelf of his wardrobe, placed carefully alongside his vests and his socks.

If I have one regret – two, if one counts my miserable choice of profession – it is that I am physically incapable of fathering a child. I am, unhappily, medically unable to perform this seemingly natural function, despite the best treatment in the world. I am, in short, sterile, and no doubt many of the amateur Freudians among you will already be drawing shaky parallels between my infertility and my career. If such is your meagre hobby, I will not complain, but model-making or coin-collecting are less harmful and take more skill. Moreover, even if I had given Celandine a dozen children I would still play the same role and if anyone is to judge me, surely it must be she. To my bitter shame, she never did, even though she was ignorant of the truth of my excursions and remained faithful in spirit to me to the end. I believe, therefore, despite George's scepticism, that she still does.

I might not be the most sentimental creation in the neighbourhood, but I do have a porcelain figurine in the boot of my car which I intend to return to the owner personally. Celandine does not forget the possessions she treasures, nor does she do things without purpose. Besides, if she *has* run away (though I am now convinced that she has not), she owes me sixpence. For the *Oban Times*.

*

The A1 leaves London at Hendon, cutting straight and north, its direction dictated by the Romans but now mercifully wider, so that one is soon cruising at seventy miles an hour through flat Hertfordshire country, by-passing Welwyn Garden City, north towards Huntingdon and beyond. At Stevenage, however, I myself was cutting out from the main stream of traffic, not easing in speed, but accelerating along a narrow road across dark earth, my car alone now (crows to the left, man standing in a field staring up at the sky), en route for a distant woodland, wet with rain though the air was dry. The wheels are bounding on a tractor path, shifting (a bottle slides from the right of the glove compartment to the left), and I am within sight of the farm and the grey stone house, and then of George's own car (a Wolseley, of course), parked, engine no doubt still warm, on the cobbles of the stable-yard.

The room I am now in (a sitting-room with a window overlooking a horseless Stubbs landscape) identifies George Holroyd more accurately than his fingerprints. Traditional, unpretentious, reliable and as dull as a ditch. There are few embellishments besides a coaching print, a James Seymour, a mask of a May fox and a photograph of Angela that used to be on the stone mantelpiece but now stands less conspicuously but still in brutal evidence on the window-sill. A sofa and two matching armchairs in loose flowered covers, white walls, beams and a pair of riding boots (size ten) in blocks, waiting in a corner behind the door. No record player, no flowers, no ornaments, no baby-pillow, but a row of books a yard long that could have been inherited from Jorrocks and probably were. When George is in the mood, and let us all pray it is not today, he will recite 'The Dream of an Old Meltonian' verbatim, every damned verse, stopping only at the line 'the cream of the cream in the shire of the shire' to praise yet again the merits of the Belvoir Hunt, his face saddening momentarily as I decline for the hundredth time to join him in the saddle. 'We could make a foursome,' he would say, 'you and Celandine. Angela and I. We could make a foursome and show them all. Show the whole bloody lot of them.' But, of course, we never did.

'Ah, there you are, Mallory' – George has entered from behind me – 'making yourself at home. Had a drink? Good. Have another. My God, you drink a lot. Do you know you were drunk at ten o'clock this morning?'

'Have you found out about Feather?'

'Feather? Oh – not yet. Give me fifteen minutes. I've only

just arrived myself. Fifteen minutes and I'll see what I can do. I'll be back then. Watch television if you wish. Reception isn't so good but . . . Well, give me fifteen minutes, Mallory.'

He then hesitated, unsure, as if attempting to recall something he had meant to add, then with a quick smile, gestured to the television set and left, closing the door.

As I switch on the set, I hear the bell on the telephone extension ring once as George picks it up in an adjoining room, then I find myself sitting in an armchair confronted by a grainy interpretation of a pirate saga that looks as though it has been shot in a coal-scuttle. I involve myself in the film, at first with the same bored detachment displayed by the actors, then as time passes and George fails to reappear, a bizarre enthusiasm takes over and I even begin to worry about the fate of the heroine, now confined, bosom throbbing, to the bowels of the enemy vessel. Rape seems unlikely at this time of the day, much, I must admit, to the regret of the actress (and to me, too) but my admiration is boundless for the villain (a dark-haired creation with the face of a Soho head-waiter) who tackles the perils of the dialogue with the fortitude of Cortés. As he descends the steps towards the beautiful but quivering prisoner, my heart is with him all the way, and even though the script will not allow him his spoils (at least before the camera), I myself will send him a rosette for a gallant try. Heroine now retreats, her back to the wall and her face registering the emotion of an Identi-kit as Don Pedro advances, ruffled arms outstretched, racing against time and the inevitable dissolve.

'I told you. He doesn't exist,' I hear a voice say, but Don Pedro is mute. It must be George, arriving in the nick of time and shattering not only my concentration but also my illusions. Behind his back, as we cut to open sea, the hero swims gallantly to the rescue. With luck, he might even drown.

'Look, Mallory, I'm not going to ask any questions – Mallory, I'm talking to you.'

'They film it in a tank. In the studio. It's not the real sea. It's a tank. He might even have one foot on the bottom.'

'On the bottom of what?'

'Well, not on the bottom of the heroine. That's reserved for nobody. If she's got one. Do you know, George, there's sometimes nothing more exciting than the unexpected glimpse of a pretty girl's bottom?'

'You're obsessed suddenly with bottoms.'

You used to stare at me when I undressed, Jay. Once you used to observe me. I took my knickers down one minute ago and you haven't looked up once from your book. Is it because I'm putting on weight, Jay?

'I'm probably drunk again, George. No, don't switch it off. I'm watching.'

'I thought you wanted to know about Feather.'

'I do.'

'He doesn't exist. There's no one called Feather that fits your description. No one at all.'

This time, I allow him to turn off the television. George now replaces my line of concentration and I study his face carefully.

'I don't believe you,' I reply. 'One man has already been killed because of him, and I'm next on the list.'

'Mallory, I tell you – he doesn't exist.'

'Someone's paying me six thousand pounds for someone who doesn't exist. Why?'

'I don't know. Unless –'

'Unless I'm a bait?'

'I never said a word, Mallory. You should deal with horses. Simple things, horses. Like children sometimes but ... You know, he might not be called Feather. I mean, it might be –'

He suddenly stops, mouth open, and we both look at each other with identical expressions, realizing the obvious simultaneously, like two scientists discovering the secret of the universe in the same single second. Only it isn't the secret of the universe, but a stupid, infantile, pitiful puzzle that a parish amateur could solve, while I, who complete a crossword every morning, couldn't even fill in the first letter. *Feather?* What devious sadist thought that up? And why?

There is no need to say the phrase but, as if in ritual, we do :

'Nom-de-plume.'

'Nom-de-plume. It has to be a nom-de-plume.'

Silence. Not even the television to break the taciturn din.

Suddenly, I wish Burbank was joining us for tea and Mono-poly. At least *he* might know what all this is about.

George doesn't say anything for a long time, staring out of the window at a tractor that has appeared on the horizon of a field, cutting across the skyline with a huddle of birds in its wake, like chattering bridesmaids. Then:

'The question is – whose nom-de-plume, Mallory.'

'I wish I knew. I've only seen his face and was given almost nothing more. My reputation as an addict of puzzles is legend-ary, but this one, frankly, terrifies me. Someone, somewhere, is playing a rather macabre joke, not only on me but also on my wife, and I'm no longer amused.'

'Can . . . I help in any way?'

'Certainly. Give me three thousand pounds as an anniversary present.'

'I'm sorry. I couldn't give you a penny. The finest and most traditional privilege of the upper class is credit. Come from the right family, mix with the right people and adopt the right manner, and you can run up bills totalling thousands. It's often all the aristocracy has left. My cousin is a lord and neither of us have enough cash between us to rent a bicycle. Sorry . . .'

I shrug. It doesn't matter anyway.

'I was only joking, George,' I say with a hand on his shoulder. 'Really. Look, George – do me a favour and show me the farm. I always enjoy it when you do that. When you take me around and . . . show me the farm.'

*

Her head is turned away from me as I enter the room, cautious not to wake her up by turning on the light. Her head is turned away from me, blonde hair on an azure pillow, the sheets low, exposing her back to the waist. Shoeless, I place my briefcase on a shelf and undress, too tired to seek out pyjamas or hang up my suit or clean my teeth. I undress and carefully edge into the bed next to her, feeling suddenly the warmth of her body and her nakedness, and so, forgetting my tiredness, reach forward slowly to pull Celandine round towards me but am disturbed, puzzled, by the rustle of a piece of paper I find pinned to my pillow. Peering close I can make out five words written carefully in black eyebrow pencil, placed in neat capital letters, three words above the other two, rather like a Japanese haiku. They read, as I look closer, I HATE YOU, YOU BUGGER.

I place both pin and poem on my bedside table and am asleep within five minutes.

*

I have been obliged to borrow a pair of Wellington boots from the groom to tramp alongside George across the fields. I seem to have spent my whole life walking by his side, and frankly, I am getting sick of it. One thing I will not do, however, is discuss errant wives, and George gratefully complies. Instead I listen as he chatters on about his favourite sport, then, receiving no response from me, he turns to personalities and we analyse Harriette and I am surprised to discover that she was once a lover of George himself. My estimation of him increases by light years.

'I suppose,' he tells me, almost apologetically, 'it's because I was so utterly despondent. I know that sounds feeble, but well ... Oh, good God, Mallory, do you have to have a reason? I know I'm not Lothario but there have been worse before me. Many. She really does have a hell of a lonely life though I like her husband, strange as it seems, enormously. But she does have to surround herself with half of London or live alone. I gave her a necklace, you know. I felt I had to ... really. Well, it was such a wretched night. In a hotel in Parsons Green ... this woman, mouth like a nectarine and that was only the *hors d'œuvre* – and I ... Pathetic, Mallory. I just couldn't. She was very nice about it and said it happened many times and ordered tea. But well ... you won't tell anyone, will you?'

'Everyone seems to tell me their secrets,' I sighed. 'Burbank, you ... and all I want to know is where is my wife and who the hell is Feather? I couldn't care less if you buggered Harriette in the Whispering Gallery – but can't you see, it's me who needs the sympathy? Today's Saturday. I have thirty-six hours, so for Godsakes do something for me. I'll even hunt with you next week if I survive, and that's a promise.'

'I thought you were going to stay with Celia Deverell.'

'I am. I'm expected tomorrow. She mentioned something about catching a ferry.'

'Oh yes. She lives on an island off the coast. Owns it really. Or at least, her husband does. He owns everything, *has* everything – except for one thing.'

'What's that?' I asked, uninterested.

'A title. It's the only thing he can't buy and the only thing he wants. Oh, I think he was a C.B.E. or something for exports, but it's the title he wants. Dangerous man, Roland Deverell, but you'll like him. If you meet him.'

'Why? Is he never there?'

'Not when his wife is. They lead separate lives. It's the story of our age, isn't it? The story of our age.'

When we returned to the house, a fire had been lit in the hearth by an unseen housekeeper, and we sat each side of it, drinking mediocre whisky. I persuaded George to switch on the television again, not primarily to see the climax of the film, but merely to keep him quiet. After two whiskies, I knew he would be back with the Belvoir and the Quorn, and after three, with Angela.

As the picture appeared (film over, villain dead, somebody telling me what to spray on my hair) George left the room and returned with a photograph which he dropped on the carpet half-way between myself and the television screen.

'That's Roland Deverell,' he said coldly, touching the photograph with the toe of his boot as if it were a tarantula. 'And I hope for your sake he's not in Argyll when you get there. Legally, he's in merchant banking, charities, that kind of thing. But under the surface, *there's* the iceberg. Everything you can name, he has some control. I don't know much about him, Mallory, but what I do know makes me fear him more than anything I know.'

I smiled and looked at the photograph, expecting to see a combination of Krupp and a piranha fish. Instead, I saw quite a handsome young man, younger than George had implied and probably very attractive to women.

'His looks are deceptive,' George said quietly.

'So it seems,' I replied, glancing back at the television screen. Another film had begun but I'd seen it before.

'He reminds me a little of Leslie Howard facially, wouldn't you say?' George continued persistently, pushing the photograph towards me again.

'No. I wouldn't say that. Not public school enough in the features. In the nose . . .'

'Oh? Who then?'

I sighed and looked at the photograph again, picking it up and studying it slowly, then dropped it idly back on the carpet so that it fluttered and landed face up again by the fireguard.

'I can't tell you who Deverell looks exactly like,' I replied quietly, looking at George. 'But I'll tell you who he is, besides being my hostess's husband. He's the man someone's paying me six thousand pounds to kill. He's Feather.'

6. A Mere Sleight of Hand

Those first church bells the next morning did not need to remind me so emphatically that it was Sunday. I had been aware of the day since its third hour, while bell-ringer and vicar snoozed peacefully through the eternity of the night, and I, light burning once again at my elbow, rearranged the objects on the tray before me for the millionth time, in the futile hope that some logic, no matter how meagre, would appear before my eyes, like colours emerging through the moist magic-picture. Place the pieces as you will and perhaps you can guide my hand, but I'm afraid we will both be failures.

Perhaps if we exchange the counterpane for green baize and the objects for cards, we could shuffle, deal and place our bets, knowing that titled personalities will now appear (unlike Deverell), profiled and front-face, mirrored at the equator of their bodies, dictating a sequence before our tired eyes. A figurine, Roland Deverell, Celandine, a club for the paper-boy, a spade for Burbank, Celia Deverell (let us not forget *her*) and, of course, Jay Mallory, who is undecided as yet whether he is knave or joker. Or even both. But there is no sequence, no order, and in the early hours my mind fails to decipher this Rosetta Stone I have set before me, no matter how hard I try, so I pace the room, smoke and stare out at the night. I have learnt only one thing, and that is that the four figures someone is paying me to kill Deverell is not extravagant at all. Not in any way. If I had known, I would have turned it down for ten times the amount. But I hadn't known and even if I had, they would still have taken Celandine away to lure me on. That I could never have foreseen, for like justice, *in*justice sets its precedents down as it goes along, like chalk-marks in the labyrinth.

It is now four o'clock in the morning and I am in a hotel in Doncaster, staring at a blue Sunbeam coupé parked between two street lamps below my window. I realize it is quite a common car among certain social cliques (familiar indeed to all Rugby players, Sunday pub-goers and readers of the *Yachting World*), but I have seen this particular model far too often. It was behind me when I left George, and its owner appears to read the same hotel guide as I do. I move away from the window and return to my imaginary card-table. Nothing. Not a thing.

I suddenly feel a fool standing in pyjamas, since I no longer have the slightest desire to sleep, so I dress quickly, take my luggage (a cheque left under the ashtray) and leave the hotel, hurrying out into the street below. The sun has not yet risen, the lights are still on and the road is deserted, and so I saunter casually to the blue Sunbeam, hesitate, then glance into the window in case any clues have been left in the occasional seat to identify the owner. There are none except that he is a member of the A.A., smokes menthol cigarettes and reads the *Daily Express*. In the front seats there is even less to attract the eye; the driver is obviously a tidy person and has left, in evidence, merely a folded road map of northern England, a bag of mints, two seat belts and the driver himself, sitting quietly behind the wheel and looking up at me with mild irritation as if I were the best man at his wedding and had turned up late. I mentally place another card on the baize table, and walk away, back into the hotel, and spend the remaining three hours till the bells begin in a mild trance, half asleep, half awake, staring up at the ceiling, my mind drifting into images of carriages cutting through fields of poppies and of Celandine's great-aunt ornamenting the deep waters of a lily-pond.

Bored and restless, I then re-read a magazine article, abandoned on the floor of the toilet by a previous resident, detailing the tragic story of a French actress who had been killed in a road crash. On one page, her face stares out at me (beautiful, alert, almost boyish and reminiscent in the bones and eyes of Celandine). It is the face non-Europeans neither produce nor ever appreciate. It is too strong and yet fragile, too independent, too revealing – not only of the owner but also of the onlooker – and too defiantly feminine. I see only the head of the girl in the magazine and she may well have the figure of a fire-dog, but she out-Eves Eve in expression alone. If her body has been left to medical science, her eyes, at least, ought to have been left to Tiffany's.

I make a note of the actress's name and attempt to tear the photograph from the magazine, but it is stapled badly, the picture tears, and I am left with half her face in my hand (right eye, a triangle of soft rain of hair, the crescent shadow of a cheekbone) and so drop the magazine, reluctantly, in pieces, on to the floor.

It is not my night. The weekend might not yet be lost, but I, for one, certainly am. Finally, in despair I pray to God for sleep and, surprisingly, He answers and my eyes close. But only for a blissful moment, as His servants, unaware that I have gone over their heads, roll up their sleeves and enter the belfry. Outside the sun has appeared, but as I walk to the window to greet the Sabbath with a soap-dish, the blue Sunbeam coupé, I notice, is no longer anywhere in the vicinity.

Ten minutes later, neither am I.

The journey, inevitably, is beginning to bore me now. Endless dual carriageways, mile after mile, mesmerizing my mind and yet denying me, perhaps gratefully, the relaxation of divining the enigma of the situation I have found myself in. At Scotch Corner there is a brief vacation for the speedometer as I cut across country to Penrith, decelerating on a road that meanders through limestone Yorkshire villages and the traces of snow on distant mountains, then north once more through Carlisle and across the border into Scotland itself. I drive fast, but within the limits of my choice of car (a Morris 1100, common as grass, but once seen, never remembered), realizing that the blue Sunbeam coupé is ahead of me, though I know the driver and I will meet again.

A thumbnail sketch of him now might be opportune, since I will soon be entering the outskirts of Glasgow and my concentration there (the map on my left might as well be in Braille) will allow me no time for such trivialities. Young, then, in his late twenties, with sandy hair and the kind of English face one sees at society weddings in Surrey or selecting ties in Turnbull and Asser. A perennial face, handed down, like the silver, from father to son for generations (tawny-port cheeks, respectable, the backbone of his country club), whom mothers invariably trust and daughters equally invariably reject as they find themselves on a Sunday morning in a soiled ankle-length ball-gown, five miles from home. At a guess, his name is Roger or Rupert or Nigel, he has a sister whose pewter-pot face has adorned the frontispiece of *Country Life* at least once, and a mummy who is now double-parked outside Harrods. When we meet – and at this rate it will be after lunch – I will try to add at least something to endear him to your heart, though I cannot promise you a Heathcliff or a Darcy or even a Water Baby. However, if he disappoints me too drastically, since I fear we will see a lot of him (the rear of his car is already in evidence) I'll substitute a character from Evelyn Waugh, since he, I suspect, would have tolerated him much more than I am prepared to do.

In Glasgow, on the London Road, I overtake him at sixty, and enter the long road hemming Loch Lomond. At this speed, and if that caravan allows me to pass, I should be at the ferry to Boronsay by three o'clock and, by my estimation, in the Deverell drawing-room (tea and bickies) by four. By five, I'm bringing out our green baize table again, plus all the cards we collected in Doncaster, and I'm going to insist on a game, or my luggage remains in the boot, pyjamas, toothbrush and all.

The man who wrote a song praising Loch Lomond obviously never left his sheep-farm in Queensland, for I have seen more beautiful stretches of water in a communal sink. It is eclipsed only by Lake Geneva for its interminable monotony and its dish-cloth greyness, though there is a little light relief in the colour of the hills and the fact that it cannot go on for ever. I am hampered by lorries and family cars (Auntie Lil sharing the back seat with a plastic devil that exhibits more animation than dad at the wheel), and find myself taking risks, blue Sunbeam ever in my wake, on corners designed for ox-carts, missing rock and loch by inches and trusting that there isn't another fool like me on the same road who happens to be travelling south.

At Cairndow I pass a sign announcing that I am in Argyll, contemplate ditching the whole affair, then cut west and south through countryside that suddenly shows its true colours; and for a moment, Celandine and Deverell are forgotten as I am transfixed by a landscape that makes me realize for the first time why the Scots fought so hard to live and die in these hills, these glens, these stanzas of natural beauty. I remember Durkin telling me he had spent his honeymoon in the Western Isles, telling me one night after getting drunk, singing *Over the Sea to Skye* in a slow, hesitant voice, telling me that when he left the army he would retire there because he had never been so happy in any other place, and that he had once stood on a hill deep in heather and burst into tears because he felt he could never be as happy again. He would tell me of his wife, Mary, to whom he had been married five years without regret. 'I will love her till I die, sir,' he would tell me, shyly, head turned away, 'even if I lived till I was ninety, sir. I know that.' I believed him, not only because it gave me at least some hope for my own future marriage, but because Durkin was one of those rare men who had learnt the simplicity of happiness. His ghost now seems to haunt me everywhere.

Loch Fyne is on my right now, slipping away, villages hurtle past and I am within sight of the Isle of Boronsay, lying below me through a comb of trees, sheep, the road twisting over stone bridges, narrow enough for only one car, a manse glimpsed on a hill, the blue Sunbeam a half-mile behind, unfolding through woods until suddenly I am above the Kyles separating island from mainland and I see at last the ferry below, resembling nothing more than a motorized raft, and I cruise, window wound down, along the water's edge to the point of departure.

It is two fifty-five, and I am ahead of schedule, though the ferry at present is on the far side of the water. A ticket-collector gestures to me as I ease the car at the top of the ramp to get in a queue that I have overlooked; and so I reverse and park, fourth in line, along the quay and switch off the engine. The throbbing in my head, like the engine, ceases. Outside (my back now to the ferry) is a small grocer's shop, the road I have just descended, a man sitting on a bench reading a book, two passengers stretching their legs. There is also the Sunbeam coupé moving past me, the driver firmly in profile as if posing for a coin, to park directly behind. We all wait, swivelling our heads as the ferry, reversing, eases its way from the far shore, carrying a milk tanker and a cattle truck.

'How long will it take to reach us?' I ask the ticket-collector as he approaches my window.

'Oh, not long, chief,' he replies in a voice he acquired in Hackney. 'Eleven, twelve minutes. On a fine day, a clear day, ten minutes at the most. Today . . .'

I am handed a yellow ticket, aware that I am being watched, not by the driver behind (he appears to be asleep) but by the man on the bench. For a brief moment I consider ignoring the stare, then realizing that I can no longer allow myself to drift in a current precipitated by someone else, get out of the car, slam the door and walk purposefully towards my observer. I am in no mood for small talk, and am in fact, as I now realize, not in my best social humour.

'What the bloody hell are you staring at?' I ask, like a dance-hall thug stepping between voyeur and girl-friend. Before me, book is lowered, closed, covered by a hat and reader looks up, squinting self-consciously. It is evident I have made a mistake. I begin to turn away, hesitate, then apologize foolishly. The man takes it very well, ignoring my embarrassment.

'You're very forthright, Mallory,' he replies with a smile. The accent, of course, is north Welsh. 'I'm surprised. Sit down, but not on my hat. You've got five minutes before the ferry arrives. Tankers are very heavy.'

I sit down on the bench, find myself facing the Kyles once more and the island beyond.

'My name is Lorenz,' I am told, 'despite my accent. Nothing sinister about it, Mallory. I'm as Welsh as a harp. We're not all Griffiths and Jones, you know.'

A brief touch on my arm, resting rather longer than a gesture but brief enough, then hat is removed to expose the book once more, removed with a precise, smug arc, thumb and forefinger on crown, like a chef lifting lid to display his latest delicacy.

'*Anna Karenina*. Have you read it?'

I shake my head, not even bothering to look at the book in question.

' "All happy families are like one another; each unhappy family is unhappy in its own way." Marvellous stuff. You should read it. I brought it along not only because I like it but because it is almost nine hundred pages in length. You see, I didn't know how long I would have to wait for you. To see ... if you arrived.'

'How did you know I would?'

Lorenz didn't answer, but stared out at the ferry, now half-way back across the water. I am beginning to lose my temper again since no one seems interested in telling me anything.

'The ferry –'

'Fuck the bloody ferry!'

'The ferry, Mallory, will take a further two minutes to reach the ramp, then the tanker will drive off and you will drive on.'

'Oh really? I was thinking of swimming across. Like Hero.'

'Leander. Hero was the girl. Easy mistake, but you'll find I'm right. Besides, didn't Leander drown?'

'Why the hell wasn't I told that Feather was Deverell?'

'Not my idea, Mallory. The client's.'

'And who is that?'

'I don't know. Does it matter?'

'It matters very much, Lorenz, since he's involved my wife.'

'Your wife?' Lorenz is now looking at me with puzzlement. 'I know nothing about your wife, and that, for once, is the truth.'

'Well, someone does.'

'You know, Mallory, I never realized you even had a wife. Look, you'd better get back in your car.'

'Thanks.'

I stand up, stare at him, then at the ferry, then begin to walk slowly away.

'Oh, by the way, Mallory, that man behind you in the blue Sunbeam is called Jeremy Atkinson. He's taken over from Burbank. Very keen, very young. Good school. Answers to me, though, if anything ... turns up.'

'And who do you answer to?'

'God? Oh – you'll see it through, won't you?'

I didn't answer, but walked to my car without looking back, controlling my anger, stopping only to lean into Atkinson's car and shout in his ear. He was listening to the car radio.

'Wait for me on the other side. I want to talk to you.'

There was a stage-managed look of confusion, then the beginnings of a protest that wouldn't get a fly removed from his soup at the Ritz.

'Now look here –'

'Shut up, Atkinson,' I continued, 'and do what I say or I'll get in my car, reverse fast and break all your pretty badges.'

The threat was too much for Atkinson, for he nodded, white-faced, watching me nervously as I strolled back to my own car, slammed the door once more and switched on the engine. First Burbank with his Monopoly set, now Atkinson in his blazer and old-school tie. I must be the last of a dying breed – the phrase, I note, is unfortunate to say the least – if there ever was one. An amalgam of pitiful opposites, striving vainly to keep myself solitary and intact. I demand no friends, do not seek them and am embarrassed and often angry if they seek me. I have spent thirty-nine years in a valiant effort to remain alone, to live in my own fantasy, shunning all contacts (even, pathetically, Celandine's) and am incapable not only of adopting companions but also (bitter joke), of procreating them. I enter. I am. And in time I exit, pursued by no one, and that is the way I want it and the way I have planned.

And yet, maliciously, I find trout in the milk, and my well-laid plans encourage not only mice and men, but cats, dogs and wives too. I am a farce, betrayed by my own nature, like the crook who was caught impersonating a bank-manager because the bank-manager he was impersonating was a crook impersonating a bank-manager. I am my own anagram, an out-of-date riddle, a labyrinth hewn out of my own desire to be free, uncomplicated and, now, most of all, wanting only to be alone and with Celandine. This whole weekend is a mere sleight of hand, concealing that card we thought we'd left with the linen in Doncaster. But whose hand? What card? And why the hell didn't they tell me the ferry had arrived and was waiting impatiently for me? I am not a mind-reader. Do they think I am sitting in this car miles from civilization, above a rectangle of wood Francis Drake would condemn, merely to measure my life in coffee spoons?

I swear, and hurtle too fast down the ribbed concrete ramp,

almost burst a tyre on the lip of the ferry, then park defiantly, one inch from a Jaguar, on the left of the now-floating craft. I notice, with elation, that it has more lifebelts than rivets, which is encouraging as I sit sealed in a car, parked on a steel floor that appears to be attempting, by the way the skipper is scanning the horizon, to circumnavigate the globe. Next to me, in profile once more (what Caroline or Fiona prescribed *that* pose?) is Atkinson, looking rather sick, still clipped into his safety belt. If the *Dhurnish* from Glasgow starts to sink, Atkinson will probably drown like a true Englishman with his foot on the brake, listening to the afternoon play on the car radio. Let us hope, if we ever arrive at Boronsay, he doesn't also share a penchant for board-games. It'll probably, however, if my judgement is correct, be chemin-de-fer or baccarat, or even poker. It certainly will not be roulette because we started the Russian version of that game two days ago.

Ah, at last land is, as they say, ahoy.

Despite my mood, I am going to add a pair of blue eyes. I feel that that is fair since Jeremy Atkinson has little else to recommend him in the way of aesthetic beauty. He's not unattractive, but I've met his type too often at Catterick and have enough to plague my mind without going back that far. His eyes, however, are quite startling, and no doubt if surrounded by a tan would melt any English girl's heart on the Costa del Sol in summer, as well as the snow beneath her ski-boots in winter. They are translucent, neither cornflower nor sapphire, and though I decided on my choice of sex long ago, am prepared to risk the sniggers to give Atkinson his due. He deserves that at least, and if he's got any sense he'll throw his sun-glasses into the Clyde.

Furthermore, I am also favourably disposed towards him (though I may retract that sentiment at any moment) since he has recognized my authority and is dutifully waiting for me on the jetty at Boronsay as the ferry returns once more to the mainland (Charon no doubt at the wheel), sealing us both on the island for at least twenty-two minutes. Lorenz, I notice, has taken harp, hat and book and gone.

I get in the Sunbeam and sit next to Atkinson and light a

cigarette. I notice that he is nervous and yet he remains quite still, after first switching off the car radio.

'My name is Mallory. I suppose you know that already.'

'Yes . . .' he replies, almost adding 'sir', but restraining it.

'Do you know who that man was on the bench?'

'Lorenz.'

'Right. Do you know why we're here?'

'Yes.'

'Why?'

There is a momentary silence, a slight stain of pink adorning Atkinson's cheek, a look away.

'Go on,' I say aggressively. 'Tell me.'

'For a shy.'

'Whose?'

'R . . . Roland Deverell.'

'Do you know what happened to Burbank? Your predecessor?'

'He was killed at London Airport.'

'Do you know why?'

'No . . .'

'Because I told them to. What then, Atkinson, is your conclusion from that?'

'I . . . don't know.'

'Conclusion, Atkinson, is that I outrank you. All right?'

'But Lorenz said –'

'Listen, Atkinson, on this island you answer to me. Do you understand? I want at least one person who will pick up the pieces.'

'Yes, sir.'

'I said I outrank you, but we're not in the bloody army now. What do you think of that girl?'

A girl had appeared from a waiting car, walking to the wall of the jetty, lighting a cigarette. She was about nineteen, was probably returning to Glasgow, and had the delicate beauty of a fuel pump.

'Not much, si –'

'Mallory.'

'Not much, Mallory. Is she . . . anything to do with us?'

'Not if I can help it. Where are you staying?'

'In the town. I've got it written down. Hotel Victoria. Nineteen guineas per week for a stay of four days or over.'

'Expenses?'

'Yes ... I suppose so.'

I nodded, then turned and looked at him, moving very close and adopting as formidable an attitude as I could muster. He was now very nervous.

'Atkinson, tell me everything you know about this.'

'I –'

'Atkinson, I said tell me everything you know about this.'

'Well, I don't really ... You see, I am to be informed.'

'Good God, everyone's behaving like children. You are to be informed! Inform *me*. First, why wasn't I told Feather was Deverell?'

'I think they didn't want to tell you his real name until they were sure you were taking the job.'

'How do they know I am now?'

'Oh dear ... You *are*, aren't you?'

'Why did you follow me five hundred miles? Why didn't you just meet me in London and we could have travelled up together and passed the time telling jokes or counting pub signs?'

'I was told –'

'Yes. You were told. Have you met Celia Deverell?'

'Seen her.'

'Interest you?'

Atkinson blushed and I laughed.

'Well,' I said, 'I'll have to invite you to tea. By the way, Atkinson, shall I tell you something? I have not the slightest intention of killing Deverell. I never had. Now what are you going to do about that?'

There was a momentary silence and I watched his profile once more as he stared, red-faced, at the girl outside. I then laughed again and he turned back, his eyes signalling relief.

'God, Mallory, you terrified me for a moment –'

'You're lucky. I've been scared witless since Friday. Anything else?'

'Yes. Well, not really ... I was just curious. What made you go and see George Holroyd?'

I moved away, confused by the question, and considered the

leather fascia on the dashboard. Atkinson's car was due for a twelve-thousand-mile service within a week.

'What do you know about George Holroyd?' I asked casually.

'Well, don't you know – that's what puzzled me. I mean ... well, he works for Deverell.'

A pause. Girl outside smiles at us, returns to car and closes door, unaware that a loop of grey safety-belt still remains outside. A jigsaw shatters somewhere.

'I don't believe it,' I said. 'He hates Roland Deverell. I've known George for years. He –'

'Not Roland Deverell, Mallory. George Holroyd works for *Celia* Deverell. He's been working for her for five years. Where did you think he got all his money? I thought everyone in the administration knew that.'

'I'm not in administration, I'm in exter – I can't believe it. He knows why I am here. I bloody well *told* him I was coming here. Look, if you had told me who Feather was in the first place, I wouldn't have had to burn every bridge as I went along.'

'It was the client's idea.'

'Who is the client?'

'I don't know. Ask Lorenz.'

'He doesn't know either.'

'Well, if he doesn't – look, Mallory, I wouldn't worry about George Holroyd. Celia Deverell hates her husband's guts. Always has. If you killed him, she'd be the first to give you a prize.'

'And what would that be?'

'Depends really on how well you get on with your wife –'

Atkinson suddenly stopped, his face crimson again, aware of what he had said. I looked at him for a long time saying not a word, till he began to shift uncomfortably in his seat, then fumble for a cigarette. Finally I said:

'Atkinson, if I ever find out that you know anything about my wife's disappearance, I will take your old-school tie and hang you by it from the top of the tallest pine on this island. Do you understand?'

'Mallory, I didn't know –'

'I said, do you understand?'

'Yes, Mallory, but honestly, honestly, Mallory – I only met your wife once. And that was three years ago. At a party.'

'What happened? At the party?'

Almost apologetically, he replied, his voice very quiet:

'Nothing. Nothing at all. We just talked about poetry, really ... You do believe me, don't you?'

'Yes,' I replied immediately. 'I believe you, Atkinson. Celandine chose her companions for poetry or for sex. She was incapable of combining the two.'

Atkinson still appeared guilty but I didn't care either way. I wasn't thinking about him or Celandine. I was thinking about George Holroyd. Reliable, faithful, good old George Holroyd. Fido's best friend. I also wondered where I would have been now if I had turned Mrs Celia Deverell's invitation down, if I hadn't gone to Mrs Harriette Greville's dinner in the first place. If I'd said no, I don't want to be a guest in your rotten palace for a few days. I suppose instead I'd probably be doing something lazy and trivial, as one always does on an English Sunday. Passing the time with papers and someone else. Someone, say, like Walter Burbank.

'Good-bye, Atkinson,' I mutter, opening the door of his car. 'It would be very rude of me to keep Mrs Deverell waiting. After all, I *am* expected. And besides, I haven't eaten for almost twenty-four hours. Not a crust.'

It is difficult for me to apologize when I know I am in the wrong. It is an inexcusable trait in my character, one I am not proud of, and which, if overcome, might have preserved at least some minor chess-pieces of our marriage. As I drove along the coast road to Boronsay towards the Deverell estate, I wanted to apologize to Atkinson, take his hand and apologize for behaving like a second-rate gangster in a third-rate thriller. I had treated him abominably, an officer reprimanding a new recruit, realizing that Atkinson, young, eager, painfully polite, had accepted my bovine behaviour with the good manners I couldn't even hope to aspire to. It is true that he had chosen this absurd profession without pressure and that I myself was still balancing on my tightrope, but so had I, and I knew that some form of camaraderie had to be established sometime between us before we all sank, like the world around us, into the mire. I brake suddenly, and wave down Atkinson's car and walk across towards him as he gazes nervously through the windscreen at me as if I were about to tear him apart.

His right window is open and I hear a pop ballad as I stare at his upturned face, stand staring through the window at those blue eyes. I can no longer think of anything to say, contemplate hurrying away but remain listening ridiculously to the radio.

'Listen, Atkinson ...' I begin, 'I'm sorry about all that. It's not your fault ...'

I hesitate, and he grins self-consciously, shrugs like a schoolboy.

'That's all right, Mallory. I shouldn't have mentioned your wife. I forgot –'

'She didn't run away, you know, Atkinson,' I begin to babble suddenly. 'I mean, not run away from me. She was abducted, Atkinson. Abducted ...'

'Yes, sir.'

'I mean it, Atkinson. Abducted. Kidnapped. That's how they work. To get me here. They *abduct* your wife. I saw it immediately – oh, what the hell made you join this damn profession?'

'Excuse me, sir –'

'Don't call me "sir". I'm a civilian, dammit. My name is Mallory. How many times do I bloody well have to tell you? Mallory. That's my name.'

'I'm sorry ... I just ... thought you might get run over standing in the road there. I mean ...'

He gestured vaguely to the cars screeching past me, but we both remain self-consciously frozen, neither of us capable of moving. My own car seems to be a hundred miles away, door still open, ten yards in front, as I nod absurdly and say foolishly:

'What ... regiment were you in?'

'Queen's Own Hussars.'

'Oh yes. I ... went to a dance of yours. East Sussex, isn't it?'

'Yes ...'

A long pause, then:

'Well, I'd better get back to my car. I . . .'

And then I was walking away, my feet lead, hating everything, and entering my car as I saw the blue Sunbeam coupé hurtle past, rear indicator flashing, and disappear out of sight as it approached the promenade of Colentray, the island's major town. Damn Atkinson! Damn him! Damn the whole bloody lot, and if I saw Celandine right now, I'd kick her bloody teeth in.

I start the car and drive calmly and carefully through the Winter Garden resort of Colentray (dead light-bulbs along the front, a bored statue, the Victoria Hotel on my right) and continue along the coast, as directed, towards the Deverell estate, past grey Victorian houses, putting greens, weighing machines, then on to open land, the Clyde now on my left. There was no question of my missing the house for it was even marked on the map of Scotland, along with other historic buildings, churches, ruins and, of course, battlefields. No crossed swords for Inverglen, however. Just a simple black spot, placed there, no doubt, by Blind Pew.

*

'Do you realize, Jay, that if Icarus had had any sense he would have flown by night. Then he'd still be alive . . . Well, not alive now but . . . Well, I met this man at a party. He was in the Hussars and I said, "Oh really?" and he said he was the Queen's Own and I replied I'd always thought they were all that way. But it must have been an old joke because he didn't laugh. Nor did you. Anyway, his name was Jeremy. I think. Told me a story. Shall I tell you it? Look, I know you're not asleep so I'm going to anyway. It's about a man who kept silent for a month before he died, not because he had been struck dumb, but merely because, underestimating the skill of his doctor, he had delivered his famous last words too early. Don't you think that's sad? He was very sweet. Jeremy, I mean, not the . . . Oh, Jay, why don't you one day, just for me, tell me to pack my things and get out. It's so hard to be loyal to someone who's never jealous. So awfully hard. So really, *awfully* hard, Jay . . .'

*

Gates, twin gryphons, a driveway as long as a freeway and I am entering the gravel quadrangle of the house. It could barrack the armies of the Great War and still leave room for the French maid. Gothic, pink sandstone exterior set among lime trees and landscaped gardens, and as silent now as a Highgate mausoleum. As I park my car between three others, a door opens far off beneath an arch and two men in black (butlers? servants? undertakers? My social vocabulary is shaky) approach, not me, but the rear of the car.

'Mr Jay Mallory?'

I nod to the speaker, the older and evidently senior of the two. The second has already taken my suitcase back towards the house. I suddenly realize that if he unpacks it, he is likely to be confronted by a Browning automatic between the underwear which might confuse him a little. I hurry after him.

'Just leave the case in my room,' I say quickly. 'I would prefer to unpack it myself.'

'As you wish, sir.'

'Is Mrs Deverell here?' I ask, glancing back at the older man who I discover stumbles under the name of Edsel.

'No, sir. They are all at the beach. Mrs Deverell will be back in an hour. She told me you would be happiest in the Portia Room.'

'The Portia Room?'

'All the rooms are named after heroines in Shakespeare, sir. It was a whim of Mr Deverell.'

'Oh yes. Is *he* here?'

'No, sir. If you will follow me, sir. We will take the lift.'

I enter the dark hallway of the house, past a pantry, towards a lift in one corner the size of a coffin. Edsel and I ascend towards Portia together. It is an old lift and slow and allows me to be curious:

'I assume Mrs Deverell sleeps in the Juliet Room?'

'No, sir. She used to. She is now in the Lady Macbeth.'

I catch his eye, hoping for some reaction but Edsel valiantly makes no attempt to embroider the remark by even an eyebrow. We arrive on the third floor and I find myself in a marble gallery surrounding a central hallway that could have belonged to Nero. As I wander after Edsel, I have only time to glimpse a few paintings, Carrara columns, a statue or two, but I am, despite my apparent cynicism, impressed. Not by Deverell's taste, however, but by his money. It's a tragedy he can't take it with him when he goes, though I myself might relieve him of that miniature in the corner when I make my own exit.

As I shadow Edsel, I hear him announce the rooms we pass, like a madam in an Elizabethan bordello.

'The Desdemona Room, sir. The Miranda, the Titania, the Rosalind. The Rosalind has a fine Stubbs which Mrs Deverell is especially proud of. The Cressida. The Ophelia, the –'

I smile and say, gesturing to the door we are passing:

'The Ophelia? Let us hope there is no bath in there then. It might give the occupant ideas.'

'All rooms are equipped with their own bathrooms, sir,' Edsel replies, without faltering for a moment. We have stopped outside a corner door (dark mahogany, antique brass handle, nothing too elaborate) which is obviously mine. I glance back at the neighbouring door and inquire casually:

'Who, by the way, is the occupant of the Ophelia Room? Since we seem to be neighbours.'

'No one, sir. At present,' Edsel replies, entering my room.

'Well then,' I ask, 'perhaps I could take it myself. I have a sentiment for Ophelia but not a drop of mercy for Portia.'

'I'm afraid, sir' – my case is placed emphatically in Portia's antechamber – 'the room is constantly reserved.'

'For Mr Deverell, I assume?'

'Why no, sir. For Mrs Mallory. She always insists on that room whenever she stays here. Are you sure you would not like me to hang up your suits, sir?'

I stand at the door (I have heard wrong), fingers resting lightly on the handle (must have heard wrong) and watch an old man unstrap and unzip a suitcase, lifting the lid to expose nothing more incriminating than a row of laundered shirts.

'Did you say Mrs *Mallory*?' I ask, my mouth dry. I am now, of course, out for a paddle again, braces and rolled-up trousers, pipe and bowler, but still, I see, untitled.

'Why, yes, sir,' Edsel replies as he leaves. 'And may I say we all like your wife very much whenever she's here. Very much indeed.'

I do not answer for a long time, for there is nothing, after all, to say. Nothing at all.

Outside, one minute later, a gardener escapes injury by inches as a porcelain figurine smashes to pieces on the paving-stones beside his feet. The damage, I overhear later, is irreparable.

7. Revelations While Horizontal

I see her first from the bedroom window as she walks alone (three others can be discerned through the trees but they are in shadow), walking slowly across the lawn, a child's forgotten Stetson in one hand, directing her gaze at the winter grass before her, and then she is below me, the window-sill making its presence all too evident, and she has entered the house.

For some reason I had forgotten her features and had believed her to be a young girl, a daughter of the house perhaps, until I recognized a slight gesture, insignificant but also shared by Celandine, announcing the arrival of Mrs Celia Deverell. Behind her, three men and a young girl, walking silently, subdued and a little exhausted (we are tree-top height above sea level), exercise over. There ought to be a dog to complete the frieze but there is not; there are, however, other features in the frame besides landscapes and figures that I could isolate, in a clockwise direction, beginning with the bonfire amid the pines (a smudge of grey smoke ascending to heaven, Abel invisible); then the sky, the Clyde, a flagpole, the baroque gargoyles of the east wing, lawn, bench plus fluttering newspaper (the *Oban Times*?) under ashtray, window-sill once more and, finally, my right hand closing the window before I myself am seen.

I am, of course, being unfaithful to Portia, and stand in the neighbouring room, a silent harmony of lakeside greens, dominated by a Millais sketch of the room's heroine (appropriately in watercolour), supine in weeds on the west wall. In a wardrobe I have discovered three dresses; one at least is familiar, since it is the yellow creation Celandine wore an eternity ago for Turner, then, for a single brief moment, for me. Seeing it here, in the oaken darkness of a room I never knew she realized existed, paralyses me. I ought to try and introduce some startling images into the text in order to convince you of the shock of my discovery (man finding the Holy Grail in the teapot, wife in sister's bed, the body of Christ in his gum-boot), but I cannot. I can only stand and stare at this empty yellow dress, in a room of rosemary and columbine, oblivious of everything else, even of my own macabre purpose. I stare, incapable of touching the material (cotton) in case it crumbles like a relic, into dust, and quietly regret the action of the figurine.

We will move on rapidly four hours (they have not been wasted for pieces are beginning to fit, though the picture I am composing terrifies me) and enter the dining-room. I have been introduced to the other guests, to the children and to the family ghost, have filled my empty stomach with alcohol and have received the honour of sitting on the right of Celia Deverell herself. The room we are in overlooks a rockery and a fountain, though curtains are now drawn, and is dominated by full-length portraits of Georgian rakes, as well as by the presence of the hostess herself, even more beautiful in an evening gown, sleeveless, exposing arms designed by Cellini. She sits at the hearth end of a table – the chair opposite is conspicuously empty – long enough for the Court of King Arthur (plus Merlin), though it is rectangular and over-laden with silver and lit by candles. Two male cousins are present, a middle-aged husband and wife (Long Island American and as masterful as a curtsy), three night-light children, two other men who view me with overt envy, obliged to be cast by the hostess as Rosencrantz and Guildenstern to my Hamlet, an aunt, a Celebrity and a white-lace pair of breasts, complementing fork and knife respectively, which belong, as I soon learn, to Celia Deverell's seventeen-year-old sister. There is also Edsel, two other servants, a tureen of consommé circulating the table and a million and one questions I am desirous of asking the enigma on my left. I mark time, however, and eat.

*

'If you had an affair, would you tell me about it? I mean, even if it was only a tart for the night?'

'It's a hypothetical question, because I have no plans in that direction, Celandine. What about you?'

'Yes. Yes ... If I had a lover, I'd always tell you about it – once it was over. I'd have to. I couldn't hide it like a piece of chewing-gum under the desk. But ... only if the affair was over. If I was still seeing another man – if, I said – then I'd never tell you. Never. Only when it was over, Jay. Oh – that sounds awful. Doesn't it?'

*

'You're very quiet,' Celia Deverell said suddenly, for the second time. 'I do hope you're not going to be bored at Inverglen.'

I looked at her, found the proximity of the other guests inhibiting and merely replied:

'What do you have in mind?'

'Oh – we're very lazy here. Drink, read, sail, walk ... whatever you desire. Anything at all. You will find, Jay, that there is always something to distract you here – no matter what your taste. I know, for example, that you have a great fondness for games ...'

Across the table I could see little sister (Marianne) watching me, a smear of gravy glistening on her chin.

'Do you find Marianne pretty, Jay?'

'For her age, I suppose I find her pretty.'

'Seductive?'

'Perhaps. But if that is the reason I was invited, it is either her or you, isn't it? Nanny, I fear, is out, as far as I am concerned.'

A smile. A brief dab with napkin on her mouth. A glance around the table in case she was missing anything. Then:

'Tell me, Jay, what is the reason that you came here?'

'Curiosity, Mrs Deverell. Curiosity. I was also intrigued to meet your husband.'

'Ah yes. It's such a pity he's not here, isn't it?'

'Will he be here, Mrs Deverell?'

'Eat your dinner, Jay. You're holding everyone else up and I do want you to taste our strawberries. I had them flown in especially for you.'

'You seem to be taking a great deal of trouble, Mrs Deverell, for someone you hardly know. George must have recommended me very highly.'

She looked at me, very slowly and very deliberately, and for the first time I glimpsed behind the mask. I was not turned into stone, nor were there any snakes in her hair, but there might just as well have been for the effect it produced. The Lady Macbeth Room was not a sardonic choice on her part. It was a gross understatement.

'You're very cold, Jay,' she said quietly, but with deadly accuracy, as she sipped her wine. 'You're very cold indeed. We have known each other ten hours altogether and you still call me Mrs Deverell, unsmiling, revealing nothing of yourself to me. Or am I being too . . . perceptive?'

'Not at all, Mrs Deverell,' I replied. 'I am merely flattering you by imitation.'

'The flattery is lost, Jay, because you see – I know much more about you than you will ever know about me. Ever. And now will you please excuse my back. I am ignoring my friends.'

I am left with auntie on my right and we share our common silence with only a polite bow to propriety. *Two Down* (5) *Is she just nothing more than a disturbed Alice?* By now, Marianne is on her sixth glass of wine (a pink stain the size of an acacia leaf now overlaps the hidden areola of her left breast) and I notice that her cousin next to her has learnt his table manners very diligently, for not only his elbows but also his hands are off the table and out of sight. Children gobble, mutter demands to leave the table and scamper off and Celebrity begins Anecdote Number One, dropping names like rice at a wedding and pausing only to pose for an invisible sculptor behind the cheeseboard.

Abandoned except for the moist gaze of Marianne (I discover later it is not selection but elimination. I just happen to be the only male in the house – apart, I assume, from Edsel and the ghost – who has not contemplated the pillows of the Desdemona Room by moonlight), I continue my perusal of Celia Deverell as she presents the American husband with the gift of an expression for his bathroom dreams. I have pushed all thoughts of Celandine, her obvious visitations to the house, the yellow dress, Ophelia, into the back of my mind – not out of apathy or bitterness (I am not yet, despite your scepticism, an android), but because another image has taken over, stronger in focus and

95

equally disturbing. It grapples for attention successfully, not only because I cannot deny the original purpose of my visit to Argyll, but because I have discarded my green baize table and scattered all the cards, like the pieces of figurine, out of the window.

Equations are now completed in my mind, questions, suspicions are being answered – or at least being hinted at. In short (cousin refills Marianne's glass, eyes partnering her breasts) I return to square one. I am here, according to Lorenz and Atkinson and Burbank, to eliminate Roland Deverell for the total sum of eight thousand pounds on behalf of someone who is not only vindictive enough but rich enough to call such a tune. I am not a detective, nor do I claim to be, but if it were the client I was seeking, not the victim, I would, according to the best traditions, seek a motive. You are now (so you think) ahead of me, and so I will say no more except that my neighbour may not be as superb a hostess as darling Harriette, but she is blatantly more imaginative and, if that were not all, undeniably more desirable and fascinating. A single smile from the lady and I would pay *her* to seek out Duncan, and if that surprises you (remember I have not shown the ace yet), let me say that before the cat is put out tonight I am going to learn a great deal more about Mrs Celia Deverell before someone cuts the string I am carefully unravelling as I stumble, step by step, through the maze.

The strawberries, by the way, even in mid-winter, are delicious.

It was the elder cousin who showed me around the house – at least as much of the house as he could in an hour without dithering too long before the ormolu or allowing Velasquez to interrupt the pace. I made all the required comments of approbation, applauded the marble halls (vassals, serfs at my side) and the subterranean swimming-pool, repeated my guide's name as endearingly as possible and elicited not a word about Celia Deverell that I couldn't have found out in a society column. Obviously, I had chosen the wrong approach, as well as the wrong pigeon, and consequently decided to change my tactics – though I was not yet prepared to go as far as blacking my face or exhibiting a hanky. After eight glasses of wine and as much brandy, I gambled that Marianne would take me as I was, without too much of a verbal pas-de-deux before entering the sheets of Desdemona, as long as someone wasn't there already.

As it happened, the only occupant of the room was the night-maid (Bianca?), who informed me before I could open my mouth that the young Miss Marianne was not in the woodshed but in the private chapel two floors below.

'Praying?' I inquired politely, measuring the distance from door to bed.

'No, sir,' was the reply. 'Miss Marianne often spends an hour in the chapel after dinner. She finds it very restful at this time of night.'

'I feel the same way about the Notre Dame,' I said, studying myself in the full-length mirror directly opposite the pillows. 'It does wonders for the indigestion. Now Chartres of course is another matter entirely. No peace there. Not even for God, let alone me.'

There was no answer, and I realized I had not quite endeared myself to the night-maid's Episcopalian heart. Undeterred, however, I continued the dialogue as she turned down the sheets emphatically on one side of the bed only.

'The portrait on the stairs ...' I asked casually, 'below the main window. That is of Mr Deverell himself, is it not?'

'Yes, sir.'

'The face is familiar. I do believe I have met him in the past week. While I was in Paris. Would that be at all likely?'

'I wouldn't know, sir,' I was told in a voice that could cut diamonds. 'I have no knowledge whatsoever where Mr Deverell is.'

'Too bad. Too bad,' I said. 'Miss Marianne, however, is in the billiard room.'

'The chapel, sir.'

'Ah yes. One floor up.'

'Two floors down.'

'Two floors down. Well, I'm sure I'll find it.'

I then walked to the door and left, conscious that the temperature of the room had dropped to zero, and took the lift down to the chapel to discover that the single member of the congregation, lit by a single candle, was lying face down on a rosewood pew beneath the pulpit and as drunk as Judge Jeffreys. Unfortunately, I myself, however, was now as sober as the Lord.

I am not a religious man, though I was brought up as a Catholic until I chose to select my own morals (if any) rather than those of a man who is not only celibate and dictatorial but also tiresomely nosy. If the priest insists on picking up his information on sex, like a pre-pubescent schoolboy, by listening to other people's anecdotes, that's his dubious affair; but I do feel that I, in turn, ought to have the opportunity to eavesdrop on *him* now and again. That quaint little hand-out offered by the Vatican every decade or so telling us all that we are equal and must behave accordingly, is as oblivious of the private deviations of the individual as *Old Moore's Almanack* or a weekly horoscope, and, usually, much more out of date. However (Marianne has stirred, dress shifting up to reveal a pair of white nylon knickers one could transport in a thimble), I have not given up my *tête-à-tête* with God entirely, though I am aware that I have broken His commandments more times than the dishes. He, I trust, still has a good word for me, for I cannot escape the feeling of His presence in the dark, empty, white-marble room, silent and cold as a Nordic forest and with the same air of majesty, despite the stone altar, the single lit candle, the fourteen comic-strip carvings of Christ's last days, four benches and the obscene anachronism of a stupefied girl in a crumpled dress lying prostrate before a pulpit. On any other occasion, I would have walked out, an uninvited guest, and never returned to this part of the house, but instead I retrieve a shoe from a font, reach down and pick up the waking penitent and carry her out, ignoring her blurred pleas of protest, and continue with this soft burden in my arms till I am back once more (night-maid en route no doubt to the ears in the pantry) in the Desdemona Room.

I place the girl amid the velvet curtains of the window-seat, accidentally creating another canvas for the room, but this time more pre-Raphaelite (a fragile white heroine against a backdrop of burgundy), then abandon her for the bathroom where I fill the tub, marble once more, with cold water the colour of an old penny, till it is within an inch of the taps. Marianne is now sought again for she has fallen under the seat, leaving only a bare leg as a marker, is picked up and dropped, fully clothed, into the icy water, enveloping her and soaking me. Shouts, gasps, feet seeking a pedestal, then she rises, a little shakily but more sober, to stand knee-high in the water, hair and dress merging wetly against her skin, to see me for the first time, watching her, unsmiling, arms folded, my body angled against a towel-rail. For a brief moment she deliberates between bewilderment, screams, recognition, realization, then suddenly, her face scarlet, she lowers her eyes, vainly attempts to adjust her two single articles of clothing (dress, knickers), regrets perhaps her motivation for shunning a bra, then her chin tilts up again, composure fights for survival, and she steps out of the bath, past me and out of the door as if she were emerging from a state coach and entering an abbey, via gawper, in order to play the lead in a coronation. Subject removes plug, follows in her train and discovers with relief that queen has returned once more to little sister, standing uncertainly in a circle of darkening carpet, fingers fumbling to find the zip on the spine of her dress. She avoids my eye guiltily, like a child caught reading under the bedclothes, then, her voice diminished to a whisper, asks:

'Where was I?'

'In the chapel.'

'Oh, God!'

'Yes, He was there too.'

A nervous giggle, then she begins to shiver.

'I think you'd . . . better help me . . . please.'

I attempt the zip but it catches in the lace so I am obliged to pull the wet rag of a dress over her head, and then throw it into a corner. Her face is white, smeared by ashen hair, white above a body that still clings tenderly to a tan she probably acquired in St Tropez or Ibiza. She is not quite totally naked for I will allow her to remove her pants herself since my passion, like hers, has been axed. Besides, I can already anticipate the next action on her part. Angling to peel down the triangle of underwear to expose the even more sensual triangle underneath, she gulps, clasps a hand to her mouth, then runs back towards the bathroom, the knot of white nylon forgotten and chinning a bottom I'd be proud to place over my mantel, muttering super-fluously, 'I think I'm going to be sick.' I catch a glimpse of her in deathlike genuflection before the toilet as I close the door and wait till she has the courage and strength to re-emerge.

I have smoked three cigarettes, drunk half a bottle of warm Malvern water and read a third of *Little Women* when the bathroom door opens slowly once more and Marianne, as pale as her room's namesake at the end of the play, reappears, a white towelling robe covering her body, walks towards the bed and me and says humbly:

'I'm sorry ... I've never been so embarrassed in all my life ...'

'Don't mention it,' I reply, offering her a cigarette. She shakes her head, stares at me, lower lip dividing teeth, then sits on the edge of the bed and stares mutely at a print of Edmund Kean.

'No one saw you. Only me.'

No answer. I light another cigarette, continue reading, wait-ing for her to make the first move. After all it is *her* room. She turns her head slightly (sister's nose, sister's chin, but a wider mouth, fuller, encouraging oral fantasies), looking nine years old in a bathrobe two sizes too big for her. Then, as if a decision had been resolved, the robe is discarded and she is seventeen again, standing over me, and for a moment I am tempted to remove my bow-tie, but the look in her eye is grati-tude not desire, for we both know the moment was lost an hour ago. I allow her to slide into bed beside me, while I stoically remain above the coverlet as she accepts a cigarette.

'Thank you,' I hear her say, but I know it is not for the light.

I nod, contemplate the jacket of the book, then place it care-fully aside.

'Marianne ...' I begin. 'Would you answer me some ques-tions?'

'Anything,' she replies, looking up at me. 'Anything at all.'

'Tell me about your sister.'

'Celia?'

'Yes. How well does she get on with her husband?'

A split-second hesitation, then:

'She hates him. I didn't realize it till last summer when we were all on holiday. We picked up the boat at Cannes for some kind of family cruise. You know? Show that we were all one big loving family and all that kind of crap. It was supposed to be a treat for me, but I knew they just wanted to keep their eye on me – at least, Celia does. She thinks I'm turning-on in the loo all the time or sleeping with half the college. She, of all people. Well, anyway, we took this cruise and well ... Listen, after two days I wanted to jump overboard and swim back to England. It was that sick, God, does she *hate* him. One day, she got drunk and they thought I couldn't hear because I was on deck, but the hatch was open and what they said to each other you wouldn't *read* about. Really.'

'What kind of things?'

'Everything. You know? *Her* lover, *his* mistress ...'

'What mistress?'

'I don't know. They didn't mention any names, but I knew what they were really getting at. Listen – I'm seventeen. Right? And everybody thinks I don't know anything. Right? Even though I've got a pair of boobs like – well, you can see. They don't give these to girls at kindergarten with their crayons, you know. So I knew, I *knew* what the whole scene was. Everybody knows ...'

'Have you ever seen any of his mistresses?'

'You mean with him? No. Look, I only see *him* once a year just about and he's my brother-in-law. And once, believe me, is too much. If he's ever in this house, which is never, that door stays locked. And bolted.'

'You mean he's made a pass at you?'

There was a laugh and Marianne sat up, oblivious of one breast, one nipple, resting on my elbow, and looked at me as if I'd asked her if the world was flat.

'Mr Mallory –'

'Jay.'

'Jay? Right. Roland Deverell doesn't make passes at anything. He *owns*. Do you understand? If he wants anything he gets it. You know that saying, "Everyone –"'

'– has his price.'

'Right. Well, he's got the price. You know?'

'From what?'

'I don't know.'

I looked at her, unsure.

'You must know something.'

'Mr Mallory – Jay – I'm very grateful to you for what you did just then and for not – well, you know ... But I tell you, I really don't know where he gets his money. But it's not from working in the grocer's.'

'Do you think Celia would be happy if Roland was dead?'

I watched her as she studied me, one hand abstractedly scratching her shoulder, then with a frown she asked:

'Am I allowed a question?'

'Of course.'

'Well, then, if *you* were likely to inherit this –' a gesture encompassing the house and probably the island – 'plus a few million pounds, and were married to someone like him, wouldn't *you* be happy if he made you a present by, say, dying?'

I didn't reply. It wasn't a rhetorical question but it didn't need an answer. In the past few hours, I realized that it never did. Opposite me, I could see the reflection of the four-poster bed in the mirror and of the incongruous duet of myself in black tie and velvet dinner jacket and a seventeen-year-old, high-breasted blonde, sitting up smiling and as naked as the day she was smacked into life. It looked like a still from an Italian movie or a fashion plate in an expensive men's magazine. It certainly looked like something they'd just never believe at the club. Or in the pantry.

I broke the image by getting up and walking around the room idly studying the sumptuous decor (jade, a painting by Rodin, a sculpture by Armitage, a photo of a pop star), conscious of Marianne watching me from the bed. The colour, I had noticed, had returned to her face, leaving white only in the small negative diamonds over her breasts, punctuated by nipples the colour of the inside of her mouth.

'Anyway,' she said finally, 'there's no chance of that happening.'

'What?' I replied, my back to her.

'Him dying. He's still in his thirties and as strong as a horse.'

'He could be run over. It happens every day.'

'Not him. He's probably got a food-taster just in case he gets stomach-ache.'

'Supposing someone just ... killed him?'

'Mr Mallory, if somebody killed him – which is very unlikely. Which is not unlikely, which is impossible, but supposing somebody did, there wouldn't be just one funeral. There'd be two. One for him and one for the fool who thought he could get away with it.'

'Sounds a nice man.'

'Yes, Mr Mallory. The best.'

I wanted to leave. I wanted to return to the Portia Room and lock myself in the bathroom and stay there till Armageddon. Perhaps take a couple of books in to read like *The Art of Survival* or *Robinson Crusoe*, and perhaps a radio, but just stay there and never come out.

'Jay ...'

It was Marianne's voice, but the familiarity of the tone cut through like a razor.

'Jay ... Look, I don't feel so sick any more. If you want to ...'

I glanced at her in the mirror, glanced at the child in the ridiculous antique bed and then asked the question I'd been terrified to ask all evening. Patience, Marianne, patience.

'Have you ever seen the woman who sometimes stays in the Ophelia Room?'

'What? Oh, the Ophelia Room. No. As I said, I'm never here. Except at Christmas if I can't avoid it.'

'Do you know who she is?'

'No. Why? Is she a friend of yours?'

'I was just curious.'

'The Ophelia Room? Is that the one on the far side? Facing the lawn?'

'Yes.'

'Oh yes. I still don't know this house. It's like a museum. The room next to the Portia? Oh yes. That's right. We used to have jokes about that. The Ophelia Room. Yes. That's the room his mistress always stays in when he's here.'

'Whose mistress?'

'Roland's. Celia's husband. Who else?'

I left the Desdemona Room just after it was light and phoned Atkinson immediately from the privacy of a telephone box at the end of the driveway.

'Atkinson, order coffee and orange juice. I'll be with you in fifteen minutes.'

'Why? What's happened? Is anything wrong?'

'Everything. We're getting out.'

'What!'

'Order the coffee, Atkinson. And don't forget – *two* cups.'

I then hung up and made my way back to the house and my car through the trees. Somebody else was already up as early as I, for I could see a man standing two hundred yards below me on the jetty, but it was probably just one of the gardeners. The Scots workman, I understand, is very keen.

*

Three months after Jay Mallory's wedding, he discovered with relief that Melanie still lived alone in her flat in Bayswater, though the objects in her room had been rearranged, startling him, so that for a moment he felt a stranger and had panicked, retreating to the door, until a chair, a book, a painting, a coverlet on a bed reassured him that he had once been at ease before them, two years before. She hadn't changed – hair was longer, fingernails shorter – but it was the same girl, for the nervousness still fringed the eyes when he looked at her, and she still retained that unique quality of appearing utterly remote, moving in her own slipstream of loneliness, eyes lowered, mouth slightly open, an alien leaf. A cup of coffee had been made to bridge the moment of seeing him once again, a postcard had been hurriedly hidden behind a vase, a flurry of irrelevant questions, a brief glance at her reflection in the kitchen mirror, before she assumed the role – voluntarily but with sadness because it was the only role she could now play – of listening to him, a handmaiden to his self-pity as he paced the room, avoiding her presence, to halt before a poster for an exhibition, studying its transitory banality as if it were a rare orchid. Out of the corner of his eye he could see her feet, her legs, the corner of the bed, a saucer standing in for an ashtray, and he wanted to run away once again, realizing not only that he had re-entered her life for a few hours merely to use her as a foot-stool for his despair, but also (worst of all) that she wanted him to.

He remembered writing a letter to her a week after agreeing to marry Celandine, writing a letter telling her that he could never see her again because that was the way it had to be. *Suddenly one realizes*, he had postscripted, *that there is a sadness, an overwhelming sadness in life. It is a great comfort. Happiness has nothing to do with the soul of man. It is a flick of the hand. Love can only be seen in the weeping.* It was precious snivelling and Melanie, of course, had never replied. He later heard that she had read of his marriage in the local paper, though there was no photograph.

'I suppose I *never* really loved her ...' he began, his eyes safely focused on the poster, 'though for a while I believe I did. Love her. Be *in* love with her. I was happy with her ... still am, but I am now grateful for the happiness. No – that is wrong. God, I shouldn't say all this . . . It would be too easy to admit that I regret marrying her. I don't. Not the marriage. Not *that* really, though I am myself that tired cliché, Melanie' – the name stammers – 'of the husband who feels he should never live with anyone. I blame her for being selfish, because, you see, she hasn't changed. She leaves one marriage and enters another, her role the same, unchanged. She behaves towards me as she behaved towards him and she ... as if *I* were a mere replacement and yet I enter marriage from nothing, the dry land is suddenly quicksand and I reach out, struggling, striking out. Her tears now herald the day. I try to be a father to her son, take him to the Science Museum, zoo, read *Babar the Elephant*. And yet she talks of "*my* son" not *our* son and I retreat into my own room, licking my wounds. Three months and we no longer kiss spontaneously and there are days I feel drained of all emotion. I shouldn't be here – why did you let me in?

'And the marriage, the *wedding* was like an omen. In contrast to that, my funeral can be nothing less than a gala occasion. I no longer see my friends, Melanie. I *meet* hers, arriving, like misfortune, not singly but in pairs. I see my name on her letters, and for two months when people phoned for Mrs Mallory, I thought they sought like mediums my mother who died long before this pitiful debacle. We are not one spirit, one body, and some days we share nothing more than the morning coffee, made by her, paid for by her, drunk in separate rooms. I ought to go. You shouldn't have let me in. If I look at you now, I'll probably burst into tears. The poster is new, isn't it? Was the exhibition good? I want to take my coat off, I want to lie in your bed, but I will return to hers and I suppose if I'd married you instead, I would be now in another room – Celandine's? – gibbering in the same way. I loved you once, I ... You shouldn't have let me in. You saw me arrive, dagger in hand, and you let me in. We went to Paris for the weekend. Went to see one or two films. Nothing I can recommend ... We never *did* get to see Paris, you and I, did we? Oh, God, let me kiss you good night. Kiss you and discard you like wrapping paper – No. More, *worse* than that. I talk too much. Throw me out. There's the phone – call the police. I love you, Melanie, and I suppose I always will. If you asked me to sleep with you now, I would crawl on my knees to you, and yet if I ever knew that Celandine even touched the hand of another man, I'd begin to die. That is how I am and my honesty, here, now, crucifies me and look, I've trodden on the saucer. Trodden on the saucer and broken it. Broken it. Broken it, Melanie. Broken it in two pieces ...'

*

The Victoria Hotel stands in the centre of the promenade, its name spelt out elegantly in blue and gold and facing the now misty haze of the Winter Garden (open only in summer), the rows of lifeless bulbs strung along the sea-wall, a yellow plastic fountain, and the bleak Kyles beyond, inhabited now by a single steamer. Now and again a naval minesweeper or an American nuclear submarine might appear to distract the promenaders' Polaroids, but not at this hour in the morning with the light low and the grass white.

Atkinson and I abandoned the coffee and left his room, and at my invitation took a slow walk across the main street to the water's edge, shivering slightly against the cold, but stoically resisting an opportunity to rest on a white wooden bench set under a baroque cast-iron roof between a map of the town and foot-massage machine. VIBRATOR. REJUVENATOR IN ONE MINUTE. SIXPENCE. Aware of Atkinson's eagerness and anxiety to hear the worst – at this hour he had shaved and tied a neat cravat – I waited till we were both standing on the esplanade itself, staring out across the water towards the mainland, the muddle of shops and hotels behind us.

'Mallory – you've got to tell me. What's happened?'

'I'm not going through with it. If I do everything will explode in our faces and not only I, but you and the whole bloody lot of us will be decorating the billboards from here to Nice.'

'Oh dear . . . you mean, they've found out about you?'

'No. But I've found out about them. Do you know who our client is, for example?'

'No . . .'

'I'm staying in her bloody house. Eating her food. Making love to her sister, being paid to kill her husband.'

For a moment, it looked as though Atkinson was about to parody Marley's ghost as his jaw dropped and he stared, speechless, at me. I lit a cigarette and said very quietly and deliberately :

'If Deverell dies, how long do you think it's going to take the police to trace me now? Even a child can see that. Phone Lorenz and tell him I'm leaving.'

'I don't believe it. Mallory – you're not saying it's Celia –'

'I'll lay bets on it.'

'Not Celia Deverell.'

'Bets. I'll lay bets on it, Atkinson.'

'I don't believe it.'

'Well, she didn't knock on my fucking door and tell me, but I wasn't born yesterday or the day before. Nor do I want to die tomorrow.'

'Celia *Deverell*?'

'Oh, shut your mouth, Atkinson. You'll catch pneumonia. Now phone Lorenz. Get somebody else.'

I then began to walk away, along the esplanade, pulling my coat around me, towards my car. A milk-cart had appeared and was slowly making its way past a winged statue along the main road between shops and putting-greens. Ten yards away, shutters were unlocked on a newsagent's office and a man (spectacled) nodded good morning.

Atkinson reached me as I opened the car door and took my arm:

'Mallory – I *can't* tell Lorenz. There's no proof. He won't . . . accept. He'll think you're opting out.'

'I am.'

'No, I mean, well, there are always h-hundreds of guests at Inverglen. And anyway, you know we'll cover you. We always have.'

'Don't make me laugh, Atkinson. You'll cover me only because you think that if the police get there first, I'd sing higher than Callas. Phone Lorenz, Atkinson. Phone him now.'

Strangely, I felt sorry for Atkinson at this precise moment, gaping at me in disbelief and confusion, dressed for cricket on a December dawn. I wonder if he ever did make love to Celandine? Hold her close . . .

'Mallory . . . couldn't you come with me? When I phone. He might not believe me . . . well, I mean –'

'Oh come on, Atkinson. I'm hungry and you're beginning to bore me.'

We both walked to a public phone booth on the edge of the port and I waited outside as Atkinson telephoned, watching his face stammering into the receiver. Ahead of me, seagulls, a sky that reminded me of Brittany. On the actor Richard Burbage's gravestone are just two words: EXIT BURBAGE. Gives one great respect for Burbage.

'He wants to talk to you,' I heard Atkinson say, opening the booth door and staring at me, red-faced. 'I told you he wouldn't –'

'Oh hell!' I replied, and replaced Atkinson in the cubicle, leaving him standing outside in the cold, nervously clouding the glass of the windows like a neglected puppy.

'Lorenz,' I said into the phone. 'Mallory.'

'My dear Mallory, we are not going to –'

'Before you say anything else, I want to tell you something Atkinson doesn't know, then when I've finished, I'll do whatever you say. All right?'

'All right, but I'm not going to believe that Celia Deverell is – well, she's not *that* insane.'

'Will you listen?'

'All right . . .'

'The success of any operation depends on there being no connection between murderer and victim. Right?'

'Yes, but –'

'Lorenz, will you let me finish! I will not say any more, but just impart this small piece of scandal for your waking hours. If wife's lover is shot, who do you first suspect? Who is the first to sit in the dock?'

'The husband, but what has that – Oh, no, I can't believe it.'

'Nor could I, but I'm in no mood for sick humour.'

'You mean Deverell and your wife –'

'Lorenz, do you get someone else or do you say – "Mallory, go ahead and shoot your wife's lover. Who'll suspect?" '

There was a long silence, a silence so acute I couldn't even hear Lorenz breathing. A small steamship passed by in the mist of the Kyles but the flag was obscured. Finally, I heard the reply, hesitant, but reluctantly convinced:

'I believe you. I know enough of you to believe you, but we have to continue the contract. I'll have to get someone else.'

'At last . . .'

'You'd better leave as soon as possible.'

'Of course.'

'Mallory – I never knew. I'm sorry.'

'Someone did, and someone *still* does.'

'You won't do anything – I mean –'

'Good-bye Lorenz. Atkinson sends you his love.'

Fifteen minutes later, I ate breakfast in the Victoria Hotel, put the bill on the resident's expenses and stood up to leave after a further cup of coffee.

'What did you say to him?' Atkinson asked. 'I thought he was *never* –'

'I told him you were Deverell's boyfriend and that I was going to kill you instead. He said that was fine.'

I turn away, then hesitate. Did I have a coat or didn't I?

'Mallory – about your wife. You do believe what I said about not –'

'Atkinson, my wife is as pure as the driven snow. I believe your every word. Good-bye.'

I shook his hand, picked up my cigarettes and began to leave. No coat.

'P-perhaps we could meet in London for a drink,' he said as he followed me down the red-carpeted stairs to the foyer. 'I'm often in the Devonshire Arms or The Apron Strings and, well, it would be pleasant –'

'No thank you. Good-bye.'

'Good-bye then, Mallory . . .'

I walked into the street once again, smiled at the milkman and discovered Atkinson, persistent to the last, opening the door of my car, self-conscious. Very alone.

'What are you going to do now?' he asked shyly.

'None of your bloody business.'

'Sorry, Mallory . . . Well, good-bye once again.'

He closed the door as I sat behind the wheel and then, just as I was about to drive off, I glanced up at him and said for no apparent reason:

'Did you ever know a girl called Melanie Amies?'

'Melanie Amies? No . . . Why? *Should* I?'

'Yes, Atkinson. You should.'

Then I drove off and that really would have been that. I would have packed my suitcase, left Edsel a pound note, tip-toed past Marianne's room and made my way back as fast as I could for London and points south. I was off the hook at last, and if I had the money, was as free as a bird to go anywhere I wished. Except for two small things totally unrelated, but compulsive enough to dictate my itinerary. The first, of course, was my own personal desire to get Celandine back, no matter what might happen – and much of it probably would. I wanted to find her and bring her back, not by the hair but by the hand, bring her back to our house and give up everything else for ever. You see, at heart, I am a simple man with simple tastes and want, in my fortieth year, to celebrate my tenth wedding anniversary with the same person with whom I celebrated the first. That is all.

The second reason, less personal but somehow more dramatic, was dredged up from the shallows of the Clyde fifteen minutes after I had left the Victoria Hotel. It was a pity because it was the body of George Holroyd and I had promised to go hunting with him sometime during the week. Now, I suppose, the appointment will just have to be postponed.

Part Two *Palindrome*

8. A Present from the Marquis

I could see the crowd assembled beside the water's edge as I began the slow descent towards the estate of Inverglen. At first I thought they might be just a group of people watching a fisherman or waiting for a boat across the river, but as I approached I could see the flashing lights of two police cars, an ambulance, one or two other cars, a breakdown truck angled across the road.

I parked my own car and walked slowly to the rear of the onlookers and saw that a small town-car was being towed, bonnet still submerged, out of the water and on to dry land. It was a slow operation, for the shore was uneven, crumbling, and the wheels of the unfortunate vehicle appeared to be gripped in mud, so it took fifteen minutes before the car was above the surface, suspended momentarily in mid-air like a marlin (one expected that the truck-driver would pose beside it for a photograph for his garage wall), and by that time Atkinson had joined me, obviously having heard the news, and perhaps expecting the accident to be my own.

I was about twenty yards from the outer ring but even from that distance I could see that there was an occupant still behind the driver's wheel, though he was obviously deader than Queen Anne.

As Atkinson stood by my side (brief acknowledgement, eyes focused on the centre of attraction) the car was lowered to the ground, the gawpers were pushed back and ambulance men and officials rushed to retrieve the body. When it was finally placed on a stretcher and carried past us, it was, surprisingly, as dry as a bone.

'George Holroyd,' Atkinson said superfluously as the blanketed corpse, face exposed, was exhibited to us en route for the ambulance.

'Yes,' I said. 'Poor old George. Fido will miss him.'

We then both said nothing for a long time, watching the whole operation with indifference as doors were slammed, lights revolved and the convoy of cars drove off fast, back to Colentray, leaving only the wet, mud-smeared vehicle, half a dozen policemen and the remnants of a crowd of self-conscious sightseers, dispersing reluctantly to continue their journey to work. Atkinson and I remained, in our separate entities, immobile, not even lighting a cigarette, as if we were in church or already at George's funeral.

'What do you think happened?' Atkinson finally asked.

I didn't reply, for I was staring at the car, noticing that the windows were sealed and the road beside it was free of any skid-marks. I never really expected any.

'Perhaps,' Atkinson said, 'he was driving too fast and just went off the ... Well, he was obviously on his way to Inverglen.'

'He was killed, Atkinson. And not by the Clyde.'

'Killed? But why –'

'– so obviously? At a guess, as a polite warning to me.'

'Oh, I don't believe that –'

'You don't believe anything, Atkinson,' I began to shout, then glanced around and lowered my voice. 'You don't believe a bloody thing. Why didn't you go into banking or the civil service, instead of this – What do you think we're all playing at? Games for the kiddies? If I were you, I'd go home and make your will and pray to God, if you believe anything, that you survive the decade.'

A silence once more. Atkinson shuffled his feet nervously, and then, as if trying to reinstate himself in my esteem, mentioned casually:

'Mallory ... I always thought George drove a Wolseley.'

'He does. *Did*.'

'Well, then, there you are. That's not his car.'

'Brilliant.'

'Look, Mallory, I'm trying to help. I know you think I'm some kind of incompetent school-prefect, but I just thought that ... well, if we trace whose car it is, we might find out who killed George.'

'No,' I replied quietly, staring away from the car and back towards the hills above, allowing my companion to lose his temper for the first time since meeting him:

'What do you mean, *no*?' he said, resisting an urge to scream. 'Just because *I* suggest something, I suppose it's dismissed out of hand. Well, to hell with you, Mallory. *I'm* going to find out whose car it is.'

As he moved away, pushing me aside, I swung round and grabbed his arm:

'I said no, Atkinson. Do you hear me? You do nothing. Nothing at all.'

'Go tell that to Lorenz. You've just resigned, remember?'

He tried to move away but I held him tighter and leant very close, trying desperately to keep my voice steady:

'Atkinson – I already know whose car it is.'

There was a snort of laughter from him, and if it wasn't for the onlookers, I might quite easily have broken his arm.

'Oh really, Mallory? Twenty million cars like that and you, and *you* are so brilliant as to know whose it is?'

'Yes. That's right.'

'Whose then? Pope Pius VI's?'

'No, not Pope Pius VI's,' I replied quietly, releasing him. 'That car belongs to someone far less notorious. It belongs to my wife.'

*

The Art of Love: knowing how to combine the temperament of a vampire with the discretion of an anemone. I quote that for no reason whatsoever, except that it has a pleasant ring to it which is probably totally irrelevant. It was said, written or sung by someone called Cioran (the sex is indeterminate) who may well have been a mysogynist, a mass-murderer or even non-existent. Like the Arno, Nimrod and Jack Tar, he is relegated solely to a guest appearance in a crossword puzzle and little else, but the quotation, I suppose, is pretty enough. Frankly, I don't understand it, but Celandine did. She would quote it at parties when the bitch was drunk as usual, and even wanted to have it embroidered into a sampler. Of course, I refused. Living with the cow was bad enough, but

I drew the line at such idiotic gestures. There were hundreds more and I'm not surprised people couldn't stand the sight of her. I could see it in their faces at dinners. However, it is still rather a lyrical quotation and I'm glad, in a way, I remembered it. One day, I must discover more about Cioran, discover and ram the information down Celandine's grotesque, flabby, leprous throat.

When I find her, that is.

*

The first blow sent the breakfast tray spinning across the coverlet to land, its contents scattered across the carpet, face down on the floor, terminating its ballet with a display of glass as it smashed into pieces against a wall, leaving a souvenir of orange-juice one would need a wardrobe to hide. Before the screaming began, I had slapped Celia Deverell's face twice more, almost dislocating her nose, before relaxing and standing over her as she stared up at me, her face stained like a scarlet fern, without a sound and also without fear. She merely waited, expecting perhaps another blow, but I was no longer in the mood.

'You can ring for the butler now if you like,' I said, 'and get me thrown out.'

'Why should I?' she replied, her voice remarkably controlled, as if nothing had happened in the past minute since I had entered her bedroom with the sophisticated manners of a marine.

'I'm sorry,' I said, 'I didn't realize that beating you up was the custom of the house.'

'It isn't. Why? Are you going to do it again?'

'Not yet.'

'Good. Then could you please pass me my cigarettes and if there's any toast left on the floor, I'm still a little hungry.'

I watched her, feeling like a chastised schoolboy, as she calmly lit a cigarette and adjusted her hair. She was sitting up against a pile of pillows that had probably depopulated an aviary, naked, except for a Japanese silk shawl (dragons, curlicues) curtaining her breasts. Opposite me, the inevitable portrait of Lady Macbeth (night-gown, taper and a muddled chiaroscuro of granite and moonlight), a window overlooking the driveway, a dressing-table.

'Well, Jay – what now?' she asked, as if we were inventing word-games in the drawing-room. Let's face it, Mrs Deverell deserves a little of our admiration for style alone. Compared to her, a monastic illumination looks like back-street graffiti.

'Where's your husband?' I asked.

'In Paris.'

'Where in Paris?'

'I don't know. We don't write billets-doux any more.'

'Meaning it's my job to find out?'

'I don't know what your job is, Jay.'

'Don't you, Mrs Deverell? Well, for your information, I've just resigned.'

'Fascinating. Now I'd like to get dressed and, unlike my sister, I would prefer you were out of the room.'

'I haven't finished yet.'

'As far as I am concerned,' she said coldly, stubbing out a cigarette, 'you have, Mr Mallory. Visiting time is over. Now get out.'

I didn't move for a moment, then I hit her again, and I could feel her skull vibrate under the palm of my hand. She still, defiantly, made no reaction. Not even a tear, saved up from childhood.

'Mrs Deverell,' I said, leaning over the bed, 'I don't know what your sexual deviations are and you may well enjoy being a masochist. But I, at this moment, am in no mood for fantasies. Next time, believe me, I'll break your jaw.'

'I'm sure you would, Mr Mallory – you notice you are no longer Jay. It's hardly the occasion for that nicety is it? But tell me, before I am pummelled to death, why are you behaving so melodramatically? Didn't you like your strawberries or did Marianne say no?'

'I suppose you are unaware that they have just pulled my wife's car out of the river?'

'Have they? The last time I saw it, it was in the garage. Do you mean the Mini –'

'And that inside was George Holroyd. He works for you, remember?'

'What George does in his spare time is hardly my affair, is it?'

I almost hit her again but I wanted her conscious. At least for the moment.

'Why didn't you tell me that my wife was your husband's mistress?'

'Ah ...' A smile, a pout. 'I see ...'

She then pulled aside the covers and got out of the bed and stood before me, dropping the shawl casually aside like an elegant stripper.

'The marks you see, Mr Mallory, are not stretch-marks, even though I have had three children. But then you wouldn't know about such things, would you?'

She then turned around, a nude model on a plinth, revealing scars beneath her shoulders and across her thighs.

'You see, Mr Mallory,' she said, covering herself again, 'I'm not unfamiliar with physical violence. But I don't seek it.'

'You must really adore your husband.'

'You probably have found out that answer already. You know, Mr Mallory, I don't dislike you. In fact, in a moment I'm going to ask Edsel to bring us both some coffee and toast.'

'I've eaten.'

'Pity. Well then, perhaps you'd like to make love to me. I'm quite adept.'

'No thank you. I asked you a question.'

'And I can't give you an answer. All I can say is that if your wife is Roland's mistress, then God help her.'

'Then where is he?'

'I told you. In Paris. No doubt at the best hotel. Whatever that is. He shouldn't be hard to find.'

'And what name shall I ask for?'

She smiled and looked at me, measuring my height, then said:

'You're very astute, Mr Mallory. I'm impressed. Try Benedict. You might be lucky.'

'Thank you. I'm sure I will.'

I hesitated, reluctant now to leave as Celia Deverell walked to the dressing-table, sat down with her back to me, cutting me out of her existence, and prepared to seize the day. The distance to the door seemed miles and I found myself incapable of moving, staring catatonically at the back of the head of the woman before me, at her bare neck, and the legs angled under a green velvet stool. A car was heard arriving outside, a door was slammed; voices, then silence, and I was left with the sound of a clock and the slow *frissons* of noise as Lady Macbeth brushed her hair. An eternity passed and I began to daydream, visions of Celandine's car sinking beneath a veil of flowers. The body of Ophelia once more, scarred, but transforming suddenly into Marianne's, her pants a nylon fig-leaf still, turning in weeds, arms limp.

'Was there anything else, Mr Mallory?' Celia said, and I could see that she had angled the mirror to encompass me.

'Only one thing,' I replied, and walked to the desk, took pen and paper and wrote four words and a signature. I then dropped the pink, crested notepaper on to the table before her.

'What is this?' she asked, staring at it.

'It's an I.O.U. for three thousand pounds, Mrs Deverell. As I said – I've resigned. If you want the money in cash, sue me.'

'Is this another game?'

'Not any more, Mrs Deverell. I'll see you at lunch. I thought I'd leave just after.'

'How nice . . .'

Then, swivelling around on the stool, she looked at me as I walked towards the door.

'You know, Jay – I was wrong. I *don't* know anything about you at all. I even left my door open for you last night. I never understood why you never arrived.'

'I don't like to mix business with pleasure, Mrs Deverell. Ever. Till lunch, then.'

'Yes. It's trout.'

'What a coincidence. My favourite fish.'

'I know, Jay. I know. Such a sensuous food. I like to see the eyes of my victims, don't you? Especially at table.'

'Will I be honoured by being placed on your right again?'

'No, Jay. Not this time. We have an extra guest, you see. I believe he's just arrived. I don't think you know him, but his name is Razzili.'

I hesitated at the door, said quickly, 'No – we've never met,' then left to return to my room to pack my suitcases and book a single ticket (economy) on the afternoon plane to Paris from Glasgow. Lorenz and Mrs Deverell, it appeared, had wasted no time in finding a replacement, especially someone like Razzili. I had indeed never met the man but had heard, of course, many anecdotes, of which at least one I could mention with authority. After his first successful year, Razzili decided to invest his money wisely and so bought shares in a chain of funeral parlours across the country. After twenty years, he has made, so I have been told, a small fortune. That may read like a macabre joke, but there is nothing funny about Razzili. Nothing at all. The lunch we are all about to receive will be, at least, memorable. Trout or no trout.

*

It was.

*

Having an hour to waste before departing for Glasgow Airport and since it was too wet to go for a stroll, I decided to make love once again to Marianne. It was a relaxing experience and also gave me time to think. The elder sister of this rather noisy girl under me apparently wants her husband removed, and so, now, do I. That someone else would now eliminate the reason for Celandine's absence seemed too good to be true, but I am not prepared to quarrel with Fortune since it allows me to concentrate on my own personal pursuit, which is to find my wife. It means of course (what a pretty headboard. Hand-carved, I would suspect) that I have to get to Deverell/Benedict as soon as possible since he is the only person I can be sure can lead me to Celandine. If Razzili gets there first, and Razzili is not a man to dither, then I am back in the labyrinth once more – I do wish Marianne would file her nails – groping in the dark.

Now then, if I leave Glasgow at three twenty I should be in Paris by four thirty. Or five, at the latest. Book into the hotel and make some phone calls – what is she screaming about? How can anyone concentrate? – to all the top hotels. The George V perhaps to begin with. Then Le Prince de Galles. Something to eat, and then by seven, with luck, Deverell and I ought to be face to face, unlike the young Miss Marianne and I. Ah, orgasm (mine) at last, thank God. Now I might be able to find my left hand again and see the time. As she is face down, I find it – two thirty-five already? Five minutes to dress, then into the car and fast back to Glasgow, past dear Loch Lomond again and – I do wish she'd stop whimpering. Has she no sense of occasion at all? – and into the plane. Sudden thought: did I bring my passport? Yes, I did. Pardon? Oh hell, she is insatiable, but I am on my feet and in my socks, so that settles that. *Now* what is she doing? Well, well, it is fortunate there are no illustrations, for her actions would get us both banned in Port Said.

Finally, I am dressed, though she of course is not. I must introduce her to Atkinson one day, if I ever see her again, which is mercifully unlikely. I am late, hurry to the door, leaving her kneeling on the floor with a face that now looks like the inside of a grapefruit. Good-bye, Marianne, I am late and will miss my plane, but while you recover your breath I will leave you with a verse in a pitiful attempt to inject some dribble of aestheticism into the past half hour. Here it is:

> Though I have touched her flesh of moons,
> She sits gestureless and mute,
> Drowning cool pearls in alcohol.
> O blameless shyness; – innocence dissolute!
>
> She hazards jet; wears tiger-lilies; –
> And bolts herself within a jewelled belt.
> Too many palms have grazed her shoulders:
> Surely she must have felt.
>
> Ophelia had such eyes; but she
> Even, sank in love and choked with flowers.
> This burns and is not burnt . . . My modern love were
> Charred at a stake in younger times than ours.

There.

Now, let me play the White Rabbit and depart, hunter in hand. And for this recent callousness, Marianne, I thank you. I am still afraid of what I will meet in Paris, but you have helped to subtract my few emotions just a little. If I remember I might even send you a picture postcard of the Eiffel Tower, for how could you know, Marianne, sweet pink-bummed Marianne, that last night I dreamt I had found my wife at last. You surely appreciate my sense of delight. After weeks of endless searching, I found her, still as beautiful as ever, of course, but alone and quite, quite dead. There were no tiger-lilies in her hair nor a jewelled belt around her waist, but I do remember she was choked with flowers and sinking, taper in hand, as if she were merely sleepwalking.

9. The Automatic, not the Poet

To my regret, the double suite on the first floor facing the Seine was already taken by somebody else. I had to settle for a single room at the top of the building that looked as though its previous owner was Monsieur Manette and this was One Hundred and Five, North Tower. It was a pity because I had set my heart on the double suite below, not because I cared too much for the view of the river, but because Celandine and I had once stayed there six months before our marriage for a single idyllic weekend.

No matter. The concierge has probably changed the wallpaper.

*

Green shutters (third-slat-left broken, a vein of beige wood) opening out on to a window-box, balcony, a cobbled road, book-boxes and the Notre Dame (we are now leaning out, shoulder above the pavement) sketched in carelessly to our right. A room of faded pink roses, re-echoed in the cheeks of the girl lying in the bed, half asleep, a copy of *Howards End* on the floor, a tray of croissants, baby pots of jam, coffee waiting on a table while I enter the shower behind the makeshift partition, and realize as the water is turned on that there is, of course, no soap. A single excursion into the street during those three days to buy an English Sunday paper, two bottles of wine, cigarettes, the soap, a corkscrew and three picture postcards of a Renoir face that were never sent. A weekend dictated by the size of the bed, timeless, sleeping at noon, a song sung by Celandine at three in the morning, sitting up, my arms around her waist and singing four verses of a Scottish ballad very quietly, and then upstaging the fifth by her tears.

Dressing finally on the last day, embarrassed to see each other clothed, wanting to take the room with us and leaving behind as we walked down the stairs not only the soap but also the absurd sentimentality of our lingering presence, wanting always to return, fearful that it would never be the same again. It never was, but the moment, we knew, could never be diminished, even if we lived in hate for the rest of our lives.

After Dominic's death, we never returned to Paris again, never discussed it but remembered it, on my part silently, as if the two protagonists of those three days were somebody else's creation. Characters in a book. They had to be, for we had both changed so much. Only once, in the last year, when a solitary moment reminded us both simultaneously of that weekend a decade before, did Celandine self-consciously admit that it had ever existed, but only by letting fall a single tear, emphatically but with reluctance, as if the tear were part of an irreplaceable but gradually diminishing collection she had acquired, like pebbles or bracelet-charms, in her early adolescence. Despite everything, however, the memory, like the room, was still there (at least with me), though, as I have said, it was now occupied by somebody else. Perhaps, after all, it was for the best, for within a second of entering the room I knew I would have had to say, turning away, that it was no longer suitable. The noise from the cobbled road below the window, I am sure, would be unbearable.

*

I found Deverell after two phone calls, disguised, as his wife had suggested, under the name of Benedict, but declined to leave my own name with the reception clerk.

Then at six thirty, having changed and added an extra item to my pockets besides wallet and cigarettes, I left the hotel (no lift, but the prices are reasonable), emerged into the street and made my way to a small bistro on the corner of the Boulevard St Germain in order to eat. I declined any wine, however, preferring Perrier instead, since I wanted no excuses for a mistake. By seven forty-five, I was in the lobby of the hotel in the Rue George V, feeling well fed but nervous, which was not surprising, and very alert. I was also aware that Deverell was hardly likely to allow me or anyone to enter his suite without being either invited, female or unconscious. 'In skating over thin ice,' somebody once said (Emerson, I believe, but check it for yourselves) 'our safety is in speed.' There was no doubt that even in the depths of a hard winter, the ice around me was very thin indeed, though the deep-pile carpet disguised it, and so it was not I, on this particular evening, who lingered in the foyer, admired the chandelier or winked at the ambassador's wife. I, in fact, was at the desk.

'My name is Kit Carson,' I said, 'and I would like to leave a message for Mr Benedict.'

The clerk performed that amusing trick of raising one eyebrow to nuzzle his hairline, looked me over with the same degree of excited animation one reserves for one's undertaker, then passed a pen and paper across the desk and moved away as I wrote:

THIS IS SOMEONE WHO IS ABOUT TO RETURN TO HIS PROPER PLACE OF AUTHORITY ABOVE THE SALT-CELLAR. SELL YOUR CHAIR, BENEDICT. AUCTION IT.

I then folded the paper in two and pushed it towards the clerk. As he was about to pick it up, I placed one hand over it and said very deliberately and loudly:

'Envelope. The message is for Mr Benedict, not for you.'

I could see the acute betrayal of adoration for me in the clerk's eye as he handed me an envelope. Casually I placed the note into the envelope, sealed it, wrote 'BENEDICT: URGENT' on the outside and watched as pigeon placed it into the correct pigeon-hole. Knowing now Benedict's suite number, as well as the fact, by the absence of key, that he was in the building, I threw a franc piece on the counter and walked away to the lift, pressing the button for the sixth floor.

It was, on reflection, far-sighted of me to eat earlier, since I had to wait almost two hours before Deverell himself felt hungry enough to take advantage of Room Service. I knew that he was unlikely to eat out, and so waited in an alcove of the corridor, feeling as conspicuous as a jumbo-jet, until finally the lift doors opened and a hotel waiter appeared (richer now by fifty francs) wheeling a trolley towards Suite 609. It was one of those heavy metal vehicles, two-tiered, with heated compartments underneath to keep the cutlets warm, and hopefully as heavy as a tank. I watched the waiter push it slowly along the grey-carpeted corridor, and then, after resting for a moment to recover his breath, check his jacket and my presence, he rang the bell.

By the time the door was opened, I was behind him, throwing him aside and pushing the trolley into the legs of the man at the door, pushing the trolley against him and sending him backwards, sending him falling backwards, mouth opening, bad dentistry, to scream as a bucket of ice scatters itself at random (wall, curtain, wall, second man) collapsing, buckling, the trolley careering across Suite 609, hitting a table (four by three) before beginning to overturn, falling momentarily on to the man, then righting itself to continue unheeded across the carpet towards the window, while I myself am now across the room and throwing open the nearest door (a cupboard? What kind of joke is this?) then another, the automatic already in my hand to encounter (wait for it) not only Deverell in a bed, but also a woman next to him, spinning round towards me, sheet to breast, recognizing me with surprise as she sees me fall, the light fading in my eyes, deflected from my purpose not by the sight of Deverell or even of his bedmate, for I had expected that, but by the sight (I am now on my knees, legs run towards me, a shoe, Oxford, accelerates towards my neck) of the brooch lying on the bedside table, lying on the bedside table between glass and ashtray, blinding me before I am on the ground, a ridiculous foetus, passing into oblivion (thirty pounds a night for a suite like this? I should be so tasteless) as I hear the blows on my ribs, hands covering my eyes, knees angled, on the floor, my face entering a discarded silk dress, and as my body is crushed I move my cheek carefully to avoid a slight scratch from a metal zipper beneath the name Balenciaga, then mercifully there is silence. I am in a womb. Darkness. That's it.

Forgive me, however, for the darkness, the melodrama of it all, but I am almost unconscious, a village amateur, not moving, realizing that all this, all this whole damn thing is such an utter waste of time. My body is no doubt pulp, but I feel nothing. I never have. I have no heart. But then you have guessed that all along, for I do not exist. Oh, God, let there be dark. Just for a little while ... Pursue the narrative in third person, anybody's, find a fourth for bridge, hang a picture, pour yourself a drink, but ignore me for a mere hour or so. Turn aside, for this does not concern you. Let that foot enter my groin for the second time without your gaze for I might even scream. On the dress I smell sweat, but no calls, no enthusiasms. Eight. The odour (I am drowning) belongs, quietly, to someone else. Nine. The blood, however, I assume is mine. Celandine. Ten. Celandine. Celandine. CELANoDbIlNiEvion ...

*

A carriage parked under a cluster of oaks, the Dalmatian wood-work of sun and shadow camouflaging the baroque motif hand-painted on the doors. Which are now open. A glimpse of leather-seating, a small ebony box, a duelling pistol by Manton lying on the floor, the hand, foot and legs of a girl visible to the passer-by. The horses (Rosinantes) have of course run away, but why is that barefooted man approaching on tip-toe, buckled shoes in hand? Does he not know that the girl is obviously dead (suicide, alas, but what else can one do on a Tuesday?), or do the shoes in fact belong to someone else and the intruder is a thief? Ah, the girl stirs. It must be Wednesday. She is nude, of course. Except for the whitebait.

*

They have blinded me. I cannot see. Not content with removing one of my ribs (are there not enough unfaithful women in the world without Adamizing me?), the thugs have also removed my eyes, leaving me only with the word Balenciaga and the ever-lingering smell of sweat and body deodorant. If I could move my head I could, let's face it, probably see again, once my face was clear of this dress, but I will not risk it. Not yet. Besides, it is dark now (I can hear a television) and the Deverell companions may still be standing near me. The woman obviously is still in bed, or has put on another dress (size 32), but it is a relief to know it is not Celandine.

I feel I have been sawn in half and the pain does not decrease. It begins to rise once more to my head, overflowing like badly-poured champagne, and I envy Prometheus. I remember the presence of the brooch, the absence of Celandine (*Where now, Jay? My feet are killing me*), the face of Deverell, then somebody moves above me, the bed creaks and the floor (poor architecture) gives way beneath me as I fall once more, silently, unnoticed, like the movement of an ant . . .

*

The scenery is commonplace and the people dull, hardly worth describing. On closer inspection they do all seem to be naked and one of them (a knight) is being devoured by hounds, but otherwise it is all rather routine. A man strung out in a harp, I see; that white face, red bagpipes on his hat and a pair of gigantic ears breached by a feather. I seek a familiar face, light in the distance, a shattered egg trunked in boats. A rabbit chewing the toes of a neighbour, a pig dressed as a nun, and who is that wretch encased in a balloon? That white face, no one speaks, no sounds except a voice from the infinite that talks of Browning the automatic, not the poet, for no reason. Ah, a river, but I see with relief that I am not represented yet in the throng. That voice again, absurdly, in such a commonplace landscape.

*

'Browning the automatic, not the poet.'

There it is again. I am sitting in an unknown bedroom. A single lamp is on in one corner, the television is now off, the woman has gone, or at least is in another room for both her presence and her dress are no longer decorating this part of the suite. Opposite me sits Deverell, on the edge of the bed, a gun (mine) resting in his hand, not pointing at me, but held delicately as if it were an injured bird or a rare antique to be appraised.

'It's a quote from a book,' he adds, smiling. 'Browning the automatic, not the poet. It's a quote from a book. Not a favourite of mine, but I remember things like that.'

I stare at him, realizing that we are both alone, the door closed, curtains drawn, my body still assembled in a haphazard imitation of its former shape but feeling as animated as Pinocchio's.

'They didn't touch your face,' Deverell continues, dropping the gun on the pillow. 'And despite what you feel, no bones are broken.'

'I am much obliged ...' I reply, grateful that I can at least speak.

'You ought to be, Mr Mallory. You could have been dead. I've ordered some coffee and brandy. Or would you prefer tea, though I wouldn't recommend it. The French have many virtues, but they cannot make amends, love or tea.'

The brooch, I notice, is still lying on the bedside table and I gaze at it, mesmerized.

'I bought it from her for twice the amount she paid for it,' Deverell says. 'But I was feeling sentimental and she needed the money.'

'Where is she?'

'You don't ask me questions, Mallory. You're in no state for that. Besides, you need a drink.'

When he stood up, I could see that he was about six foot two and with the kind of body one sees in exclusive clubs or on the terrace of a Mediterranean patio. Lean, finely muscled and over-tanned. Thinning hair, which didn't seem to bother him for he made no attempt to disguise it, narrow shoulders, silk shirt and linen trousers. Bare feet. I expect, if I was in the mood, I would think him quite likeable, but I had not only read too much about him, I was also, like his wife, unimpressed by his own personal pursuit of pleasure. I decided therefore to say nothing, drink the coffee and brandy (Rémy Martin, a personal favourite) and listen. Roland Deverell, I soon discovered, liked a captive audience.

'Jay Mallory,' he said casually, as if reading a title from a book on somebody's shelf. 'Married nine years to Celandine-Dora Mallory. No children, except one stepson, now, regrettably, buried. Private assassin, who was once considered a model of his class but couldn't now hustle a job in the Congo. A little overweight, a little out of date, a little overdrawn. At the bank. Impressive past. Unimpressive if somewhat limited future. If you were a horse, you'd have been put out to pasture years ago and would probably be under it. End of biography.'

'You seem to know a lot about me,' I said as Deverell idly

pulled on a pair of black socks, carefully smoothing out the creases.

'Oh, I do, Mallory,' he said. 'I even know who employs you. I don't mean your client, but who you work for. At the top.'

I looked at him, puzzled. Suddenly a mood of amiability had entered the room, as if we were both at a picnic or chatting on deck-chairs during a cruise. I felt I could almost stand up, say good-bye and leave, probably even borrow money for the fare home. He had produced that kind of effect, without effort, and I wasn't surprised that everybody hated him. Charm such as his ought to be shared around with the biscuits, a morsel for all, not monopolized by the host. Strangely, however, as I sat there, immobile, frightened to move a limb in case it fell off, I myself couldn't dislike the man, despite the fact that not only had he almost beaten the life out of me, but he had also (the lungs ache) made love to my wife.

'Lorenz,' I said quietly. 'I work for Lorenz.'

'No,' he replied with a gesture one reserves for mosquitoes, then proceeded to put on a pair of shoes, removing the trees from inside, and sliding the shoes onto his feet with casual precision.

'Lorenz,' I repeated.

'I said no, Mallory. Didn't you hear me? Next time you buy a pair of shoes, buy these. Muraschi. Never need polishing. They're Italian but otherwise . . .'

He then smiled and stood up and looked at me, his head at an angle.

'What size do you take?'

'Nine and a half.'

'So do I. Take them.'

He then removed the shoes and placed them carefully, side by side, on a table near my elbow.

'Very good condition. And only one owner.'

He then smiled again, found another pair of shoes (black), put those on and said, his back to me:

'Do you know who you work for, Mallory?'

'*You* tell me.'

He turned and replied:

'I will. You work for me. You always have. Now isn't *that* a coincidence?'

At that moment, as if rehearsed, in order for me to recover my composure, the door opened and the woman I had seen for a brief moment earlier in the bed entered the room. She was now wearing the Balenciaga dress, though the zip at the back was undone (no bra, a triangle of back the colour of sand), and held an unlit filter cigarette between her lips. Without looking at me – in fact ignoring me to the point of impertinence – she crossed the room, picked up a lighter, lit her cigarette, turned, hesitated for a moment before Deverell, then shrugged and left the room, closing the door once more.

'I have a film of her,' Deverell said, gesturing towards the closed door, 'that I made myself in this very room. It is only sixteen millimetre and black and white, I'm afraid, but in it she is being raped and beaten by three men. Dalmas, out there, was one of them. During it, I keep the camera solely on her face. Just her face, except for the final moment when I pan – I think that's the word, Mallory – pan down her body and reveal the carnage. It's quite a remarkable film and the sounds are un-believable. And yet, she still stays here with me. Does that sur-prise you?'

'No.'

'No? Well, there you are. Her name's Melanie, by the way.'

'Yes, I know,' I said. 'We've met before.'

'Oh yes. Small world.'

'Can I go now?'

'Yes. On one condition. Tell me why you came here.'

'Don't you know?'

'To kill me, it appeared.'

'Not quite. I was asked to, but I resigned.'

'Very wise, Mallory. Women are extraordinary creatures, aren't they? You know – I never realized she hated me that much.'

'How do you know it's a woman?'

'Mallory, you have probably realized by now that I am not as naive as I look. Besides, who else but Celia can profit by it and know where to find me so easily?'

'Can I go now? I'm very tired.'

'You haven't told me yet why you came here?'

'To find my wife.'

'Ah, that's what the message meant. Well, she's not here.'

'I know. But you could know where she is.'

For a moment, I thought Deverell was going to be sick, for he turned his back on me suddenly and leant against the walls, arms doubled up across his chest. Then, suddenly, as if nothing had happened, he walked to the door, opened it quickly and said to one of the two men who were sitting on a rather faded chaise-longue that looked Regency but was probably fake:

'Dalmas, accompany Mr Mallory home.'

The taller of the two men stood up and glanced at me. His Oxford shoes, I noticed, had been recently cleaned.

'I can manage,' I said, attempting to stand up, forgetting the condition of my health, then collapsing back into the chair in agony.

'Accompany Mr Mallory home, Dalmas. Take the Buick.'

Slowly, unaided, I got to my feet again, then, allowing Dalmas to support me, walked to the door of the suite, past Melanie (eyes averted, hand making curlicues in the ashtray with the cigarette), past the second man, past the trolley, now in a corner, and out towards the corridor. As I reached Deverell, he touched my arm and said quietly:

'Meet me tomorrow at the Polatouche for breakfast. We might have something to talk about.'

'No thank you.'

'Not too early. About nine thirty. Good night, Mallory.'

Eight minutes later, Dalmas and I were in the underground garage of the hotel and walking towards a large Buick in a far corner. My body had now begun to function again, but the pain was still there. As we reached the car, however, I stopped at the driver's door and turned to Dalmas:

'Mr Deverell suggested I should drive. You see, I know the way and I'm a very bad passenger.'

Dalmas hesitated, unsure. We were not, after all, the most intimate of friends.

'Go on up and ask him,' I said casually, 'but I warn you, you're not in his best books tonight. You see, you hit the wrong man.'

I smiled and held out my hand for the keys.

'Now be a good boy, Dalmas, or I'll have to report you when your employer and I have breakfast tomorrow.'

I thought for a moment that Dalmas was more intelligent than he looked, but by good chance he didn't even possess the instinct of Fido, and the keys were dropped solemnly into the palm of my hand. Immediately I am sitting behind the wheel of the car in the empty garage, grateful that there is enough room for me to reverse fast before my passenger has even time to walk round the bonnet to his own seat. I then braked, pushed the gear into Drive and accelerated so fast that I hit him before he had even time to run. I felt the full weight of the Buick (a '68 model, four-door, painted a rather pleasant shade of olive green) go over Dalmas's body as he fell under the offside wheels (two bumps) before I was spinning the car round and out of the garage and into the street, regretting only the fact that my other assailant had not generously offered to take me home as well.

It was a thought that irritated me all the way back to my hotel, so it is not surprising that it wasn't until I stepped on to the pavement that I realized that I'd forgotten to switch on the car lights. It was an absurd oversight on my part and I was very fortunate that no one noticed, for in Paris, I believe, one can be booked and fined on the spot, no matter what the excuse, for an offence as trivial as this.

As if the day had not been pleasant enough, however, another incident took place – though *incident* is perhaps the wrong word – before I was finally allowed to enter a voluntary sleep.

Entering the hotel, I was suddenly surrounded once again, despite the pain in my body, by memories of Celandine. This door, that plaster urn, that mirror in the lobby had been there far too long, and even the flowers (plastic) seemed the same ones we had both passed as lovers a decade ago en route to our bed. Foolishly nostalgic as well as feeling suddenly very alone, I dreaded the night in the attic (oh, no – I've forgotten the shoes!) and so approached the night-clerk. Before speaking, I placed twenty francs on the desk, tucking the note into the corner of the blotter and said casually in sub-title French :

'The double room on the first floor front. I know it is taken, but perhaps the occupants could be moved.'

The money was studied, then the donator (dried blood, by the way, still clings to my shirt), but there was no answer. Undeterred and realizing that I was in Paris, I appealed to the man's sense of romance. Bitter mistake. I had forgotten that the last two Romantics to live in France were a homosexual from Reading Gaol and a Jewish painter from Leghorn, and so (I am now audacious) a further twenty francs. Eyes are now raised from the magazine and Cerberus speaks. I am told that it is impossible for the hotel to remove the occupants since the occupants have not yet arrived.

'Then when they arrive,' I say, thrusting the forty francs into the clerk's top pocket, 'put them in another room. They'll never know the difference.'

'The occupant insists on that room, monsieur. And he arrives tonight.'

'Well then, perhaps I could speak to him myself. Explain the situation. What is his name?'

'Razzili, monsieur.'

Without another word, I retrieve the forty francs and return to my attic. There are some days, I have been told, when nothing ever goes right. Besides, I am sure in time I could grow quite fond of my little room. At least it is quiet and remote, and no one will hear me when I wake up screaming.

10. A Fine Day for Flying a Kite

When I opened my eyes the next morning, I was mildly surprised to discover not only that my skin had been redecorated in parts the colour of a damson, but that I was also soaking wet. The bruises I could account for and probably learn to live with, but the hole in the roof above my bed I could not. There must be less inconvenient ways of finding out that it has rained during the night, and at three pounds a day one expects a certain amount of luxury. Even in a garret in Paris. The only consolation was that the water (it is still pouring through, believe me, for I can see it now) had woken me up in time to make the rendezvous with Deverell. I didn't care too much for his company, but at least the breakfast would be on *his* bill. Consequently, after complaining to the concierge, dressing in my only other suit and demanding that an umbrella be placed in the attic, I set off as best I could towards the Polatouche, taking the Metro since the Buick, I noticed, had mysteriously disappeared while I slept.

The restaurant, as I anticipated, was not, thank God, one of those fashionable market-places so highly praised by Lucrezia Borgia and the social cliques of every city, but a small, expensive and exclusive bistro in the wrong part of the town, in which only the patron and his wife, and now and again a distant cousin from Nantes, appear to eat. Otherwise, empty, secretive and known only to the delivery boy, the postman and, of course, Roland Deverell. He was sitting in a far corner booth, apparently dressed for a funeral, and reading the comic strips in the *Herald Tribune*. Before him was an empty bowl of coffee, an ashtray with two stubs of the same brand of cigarette and a clean cup and saucer for me.

'You're early, Mallory,' he said as I sat down, not opposite him but next to him, so that we both faced the door. I didn't

reply but pulled the cup towards me, allowing it to be filled by
the owner, who hurried away again immediately, then lit my
first cigarette of the day.

'You forgot your shoes,' Deverell said, folding the paper and
placing it carefully on the table by his elbow. I could smell
Prince Gourielli after-shave, stronger than the coffee, and then
caught my own reflection in a mirror across the restaurant. The
image was far from flattering and though Deverell was right
when he said that my face was untouched, I looked as if I had
modelled my appearance on a scarecrow.

'I know,' I replied, sipping the coffee. 'Give them to Dalmas.'

'I can't. He was run over by a car.'

'I'm sorry to hear it.'

'So am I. He's still alive. It's going to cost me a fortune in
hospital bills.'

'You should have had him insured against such things.
Private ward?'

'Of course not. We must be democratic about this, even in
France.'

'I feel the same way. Are you paying the bill? For the breakfast I mean.'

'I thought we'd go Dutch.'

'I'd rather not. Muraschi shoes are one thing, but I draw the
line at wearing clogs.'

'Do you always talk like this?'

'Like what, Deverell?'

'Like – Oh, drink your coffee. When you've finished that, we
can behave like human beings.'

The coffee, naturally, was delicious. I have known gourmets
all over the world who have tried to emulate Parisian coffee and
always failed. Perhaps, one surmises, it is not the actual coffee at
all, but the city air that injects the right mixture of flavour and
refreshment in a simple beverage like a cup of coffee. And if
that sounds like an advertisement, I make no apologies. Celandine used to make good coffee, but it was Brazilian or Cuban,
not French, though the character was there. I wonder why she
had to sell the brooch?

'You know, Mallory,' Deverell said, lighting yet another
cigarette, 'I suppose I'm basically a misogynist. That doesn't

mean I hate women, though most of them I wouldn't tip my hat to. If I had a hat. But now and again, one meets a woman who so devastates one, who is so disturbingly enticing, a butterfly resting on the opposite shore, that one wants to cage her up, pin her to a board in case she escapes. I have met only two women like that in all my life. Both of them hate me and both of them are, regrettably, married. One to me. And the other – drink your coffee – to you. Life is full of such coincidences, isn't it?'

'Like Melanie.'

'Melanie. Oh . . . Mel-a-nie. Deflowered by you, buttonholed by me. Melanie. Yes. But Melanie, I'm afraid, came with the suite like the television set, the ice-bucket and the Michelin Guide. She is to be kept in the games cupboard to be employed when bored, like mah-jongg or chess or Scrabble.'

'Or Monopoly.'

'Yes. Or Monopoly. Burbank played Monopoly, didn't he? Remember him, Mallory? You know we were very grateful to you for telling us about Burbank. It was a rare and touching gesture.'

'Do you know where Celandine is?'

'I could find out.'

'And would you tell me?'

'Not yet.'

I stood up to leave, the coffee unfinished, but didn't even reach the door. It was a melodramatic gesture at the worst of times, for Deverell didn't even try to stop me. These things, I assume, only happen in pre-war plays. I order more coffee and sit down again.

'Mallory – I love your wife very much.'

'So do I,' I replied. 'So why don't you stick to your own possessions? She's all I have.'

'But Celia would like me dead.'

'That's the understatement of the age. Where's Celandine?'

Deverell smiled and leant back in the corner of the booth and stared out at the rain through the restaurant window. He looked very young, almost adolescent, like an English poet in the Great War. If only there was something about him I could hate, but it was impossible and I cannot (and, God, how I've tried) explain why. I suppose, in a way, we were both too much alike, even in our choice of women. Except that he was a success and I ... Well, let us not get maudlin for the croissants have arrived.

'Mallory ... It's a ... it's a shock to suddenly find out that someone you once lived with, made love to, shared your secrets with, wants you dead. It's quite a shock.'

'Where's Celandine?'

'Listen, Mallory, I will tell you – not now. Not here. Not yet. I will tell you after you do something for me. In exchange. I will then tell you where she is. I will even let you have her back, if she wants you. I promise.'

I looked at him, but he didn't avoid my eye and I realized, falteringly, that he really did love Celandine – perhaps even more deeply than *I* had ever done. A long time passed, the croissants were eaten, fingers were wiped, we posed like Degas's absinthe drinkers and then I said:

'Tell me first – does *she* love you?'

'That, Mallory, you'll have to find out for yourself. Do you remember a poem she used to quote? Do you remember? In that soft, blurred voice of hers:

> 'And she will wake before you pass,
> Scarcely aloud, beyond the door,
> And every third step down the stair
> Until you reach the muffled floor –'

*

'Will laugh and call your name, while you – Jay, you're not even listening.'

'I was watching the kite.'

It was Japanese, I think, and therefore unused to the Berkshire Downs. The wind was high but uneven, reluctant to join in the sport as Dominic (red shirt, corduroys, sandals) clung grimly to the spool, running through the long grass, head angled back to watch the octagon of dragon at the end of the line dip and hover only inches above his face. At one point, encouragingly, it attempted to soar but Dominic was no longer in sight, having fallen amid nettles before reappearing, eyes wet with tears, to run past my outstretched hands, past me and into the arms of his mother. Soothing him with a boiled sweet, she continued, book on lap, one hand holding down the flapping pages:

> – while you
> Still answering her faint goodbyes,
> Will find the street, only to look
> At doors and stone with broken eyes.

'Shall I go on?'

'What?'

'I said shall I go on reading? Oh, for Christ's sake, Jay, why are you so insensitive?'

'I'm not insensitive. I was just looking for Dominic's kite. It took me an hour to make it and now it looks as though it's blown away.'

'I wouldn't worry, Jay. You can always make another one with a page from this book. Any page. Any page will do. They're all the same. Aren't they? Well – *aren't* they?'

*

'Let's get out of here, Mallory. This place is too familiar.'

'You took her here, too?'

'Yes . . .'

'I haven't finished my coffee.'

Deverell hesitated, looked down at me and then said, very quietly, placing a note to cover the breakfast on the marble table-top:

'Now I know why she left you, Mallory. You haven't got an atom of emotion in your whole body. You only dream that you do. You never even saw her. You never even saw her at all. Not once.'

'She never left me, Deverell. You took her away.'

'She left you, Mallory. She left you five years ago. She lived with you, but she left you. Her departure last week was just a mere formality.'

'Are you saying she hates me?'

Deverell picked up the newspaper and placed it in his pocket, glanced at the mirror, then, pushing past me, said:

'No, Mallory. She doesn't hate you. I wish she did. But she doesn't. I know that now.'

He then walked slowly to the door of the restaurant, nodded to the patron and waited on the pavement, staring into space until I'd drunk the coffee and finished my cigarette. I took my time, even though he was standing in the rain, and when the change from the bill was placed on the table, I took it all and put it in my pocket, for I had noticed, unlike Deverell, that the menu said quite clearly, and quite emphatically, that the service was *compris*.

Paris is now below us, below us and ignored as we both stand on the white parapet decorating the apron of Montmartre. Behind us, steps, level, steps, road, Sacre-Cœur. Above, grey sky. Nothing more; though other visitors (you, perhaps) may write endless letters home describing the beauty of such a familiar place (remember the painting by Utrillo?), I am content merely to place myself and Deverell in the appropriate location, chosen by him, to continue our conversation. Like the Taj Mahal and the pyramids, any adjective, adverse or favourable, prefixing the name of the landmark can only be superfluous. It has, however, stopped raining.

'Wretched city,' said Deverell, staring down at the roofs below. 'I ought to hate it but I don't. Look at it.'

'Tell me what you want me to do. I'm cold.'

'Yes . . .'

Deverell moved closer, not looking at me, but leaning over the parapet, gazing at the horizon below. When he spoke, it was in a voice so low that I had to strain to catch the words and only then by moving closer to him, so that our shoulders were touching and I was inches away from his profile.

'I'm not afraid of death, Mallory. Not of death itself. As somebody said — all I desire for my own burial is not to be buried alive. No, I feel nothing about that. About death. But of dying . . . Then I hesitate. My wife used to ridicule me by saying that I would not allow myself to die until Burke allowed me into his *Peerage*. But that's a fallacy. A passing whim. I'm searching for words, Mallory. I know I have enemies. I always have had. Some I know would be happy to attend my funeral.

141

They would even hire morning suits and wear a carnation. But till now, till you arrived, I didn't know that I had been chosen as a victim. Specifically. Chosen ... A target. You resigned, but after you there must be somebody else. Then if he fails, somebody else. Like a Sicilian vendetta. She will never stop now. The hatred is too deep.'

I didn't reply, waiting for him to ask the inevitable:

'*You* know, Mallory, who has taken your place, don't you?'

'I might.'

'You do know. You're not a fool. Give him to me and I'll tell you where – no, I'll find out where Celandine is.'

'But if I give him to you, what about the next? You said so yourself. There'll be another.'

'Give me your successor, first. He's too close. Give him to me.'

'And if I do, how do I know you will keep your word? How do I know you will not kill *me*?'

Deverell smiled and looked at me.

'I won't. I assure you of that. Besides, I'll need you for an assignment. Oh – giving me your successor is not an assignment. You will have to do nothing. You'll just tell me who and where he is and I'll do the rest. No, after that, then, Mallory, *then*, I'll need you.'

'The horse in the pasture?'

'The horse in the pasture. But you'll be a very rich horse. And you'll never have to work again. You can settle down with your wife and have kids – well, you can adopt them perhaps.'

'What is the assignment?'

'To go back to the source. What else, Mallory? One has to get rid of the source. I assume you don't object to killing women?'

The man is insane. In all my life, I am hard put to think of anything that might redeem my own conscience, but I have yet to encounter a callousness as horrifying as is now being exhibited by Roland Deverell. He is telling me to kill his own wife as if it were just another move in a chess game, telling me so casually, as if I were as heartless as he was. I want to throw up. No doubt I have not endeared myself to your bosom and I know that by now you are unlikely to invite me to your garden party in July or to attend your daughter's christening (which is a pity) but even I, pitiful creature that I am, have principles. I have never, believe me, killed a woman. Indeed I have never killed anyone who has been anything but a stranger to me. My dossier is not my address book, and if I were to meet my victims in the smallest of rooms, I would be hard put to remember even one of their Christian names or their favourite view of Boulogne. I am alive because of this and now, here, before a church, God help us, I am being asked not only to execute a woman (beautiful, sophisticated coriander) but a woman whom I know and who had the kindness to feed me imported strawberries. In order to prove what kind of man I am there is only one thing I can say to this creature on my right, regardless of how dangerous he is, and I say it without fear or hesitation:

'How much?'

'Eight thousand pounds?'

'Ten.'

'Done.'

We then shook hands and walked away – he to have lunch with Melanie and I to have a quiet *tête-à-tête* with Emilio Razzili.

11. Enter Harpies

The room was almost the same. I had gone there two hours after leaving Deverell, forgetting that I was about to re-enter that room, that faded snapshot of my past, and for a moment I could only stand stupidly at the door, oblivious of the man in the chair, and gawp at the bed, the single painting, the green shutters opened out on to a single cube of the Seine. Nothing had changed, not a thing, reminding one of a familiar painting (interior, unknown artist, one of several) one had lived with as a child, lost, then rediscovered by chance in a trunk below the stairs. One is not surprised by the discovery, but more by the fact that the picture, unlike oneself, has not altered in any way except perhaps that one's maturity has given it a malicious veneer of criticism. The chair now is out of proportion, the colours clash and the man (a new addition in a black mohair suit) seems abnormally lifeless. Like a waxwork dummy, except that Razzili is unlikely to be invited to Madame Tussaud's. Moreover, he is at present very much alive, is smoking a cigar (Dutch) and wears, besides the mohair suit, a white shirt, black tie, black shoes and a pair of reading glasses as he studies a map of the city. He doesn't even look up as I enter, though I have knocked twice, but he is not unaware of my presence. Even the ashtrays are the same, surprisingly, though I trust they have changed the sheets. Ten years is a long time.

Quieter ... Just there. There, Jay. Chickadee is dreaming of Bosch. There, Jay, chickadee is dreaming, dreaming of Bosch.

I sit on the edge of the bed studying Razzili, who totally ignores me. He knows who I am because we dined at Inverglen, but then he said hardly a word, and made not a single movement that was in any way superfluous. I doubt if he even sweats. He is precise, exact, even in his choice of features. The nose is straight, eyes and teeth are regular and the hair is straight and combed in the manner of the silent-film stars of the nineteen twenties (though parted to the side rather than in the middle), lying flat to the head, and unimpeded by a curl or an encroachment over the forehead. An unimpressive man, certainly, to look at, though he may photograph well in monochrome, but not a man I would care to offend, even in the slightest way. Consequently, with Razzili, and like Razzili, one treads warily.

'You remember who I am. My name is Mallory. We met at Boronsay.'

There is no answer. He is concentrating on Neuilly.

'I know why you are here, Razzili. I know who sent you and I know what you are paid to do. So does Deverell.'

Still no reaction. I might as well be talking to the wall and probably am.

'Listen, Razzili, I want to help you. I am not employed to, but my reasons are personal. I want to help you get rid of Deverell. He has tried to bargain with me and as far as he is concerned I have accepted his bargain, but I'd rather have him dead. And you can't do it alone. Do you hear me, Razzili?'

I was now rewarded by a slight movement from the occupant of the room as he walked to the door of the toilet, entered and closed it. After two minutes, I heard the sound of water being flushed, then Razzili came back, resumed his original pose in the chair and returned to his map. We were back it seems to square one.

'Razzili – whatever Celia Deverell told you, her husband is no longer living under the name of Benedict. You cannot find him. Furthermore, he knows you are here and you are being followed. By tonight, you'll probably be dead. Unless you listen to me.'

Silence. I stared at him, then sighed, stood up and left the room. That was it. There was nothing more I could do. Goodbye ten thousand pounds.

An hour later, I am lying on my bed in the attic – it has been moved clear of the sky – reading a magazine and contemplating packing my suitcase, when the door opens and I am face to face once more with the occupant of the first-floor-front double suite.

He stands and surveys the room, then studies me, then the hole in the ceiling, the view from the window and finally says:

'What do *you* make out of this?'

'It's none of your business,' I replied. 'I said it was personal.'

'I want to know what it is.'

'Why?'

'Because I don't trust you, Mallory.'

'I don't trust you either. But I want Deverell dead.'

'Why?'

'I've told you. Personal reasons.'

'Money?'

'No.'

'If it's not money, then he must have fucked your wife. What else?'

Calm down, Mallory. By the end of the day, this man in front of you might be no more. Calm down.

'I didn't invite you here, Razzili. You're in my room now.'

'Who told Deverell I was here?'

'I did.'

'Why?'

'To gain his confidence. I even told him I would give you to him and I will unless you listen to me. He wants to kill you, Razzili, and he can and will. There's probably a bomb in your room right now and prussic acid in your tap-water. You see, Roland Deverell is the chairman of the board. *Our* board. Or did Celia not mention that small fact?'

I could see Razzili hesitate, unsure, watching my eyes which were carefully focused on the sink-plunger breasts of a starlet on page 39.

'If I accepted your help,' he said finally, 'what will you tell me?'

'That if you want to stay alive and collect your money, you'll have to get Deverell first. Tonight. And I know where he will be.'

'Where?'

'His girlfriend has expensive tastes in clothes.'

'So?'

'Stay in your room, Razzili. Till this evening. Put on a black tie and I'll call for you at eight.'

'I still don't trust you.'

'That's your privilege. Black tie, remember. It'll be very smart.'

Razzili then left the room, leaving me alone once more. I didn't go out for the rest of the day, except for one minor excursion to collect some cigarettes and make a single telephone call to Roland Deverell, then I returned to the attic, lay on the bed and stared at the wall. I have lost my ability not only to concentrate but also to think. I have become an inanimate object. I sit, lie, like an Eastern mystic, draining the emotion from my body, slowly enabling myself to prepare, not for the evening's fashion show, but for the death of Celia Deverell. A week ago, less, I could not have even contemplated the idea of the act, but now . . .

To say that I am not nervous would be a gross falsehood. Of course I am. But the equation (you note how lately my imagery is mathematical. My style too has lost its romance and I talk of Celandine less) is as basic as $E = mc^2$. Whatever moment it is in the life of man when he makes a decision is irrelevant. The choice, however, is his. Puerile statements, I gibber on in a room that couldn't even contain a string quartet, minus bass fiddle. And yet, I am confronted by the basic issue – my next assignment will be my last. It will also reintroduce me to Celandine – that I can promise you, for all who like a happy ending – after I have erased the wife of my superior officer. If I fail, Celia will remain alive and I will be dead. There are no other permutations – except one, and that I care not to think about. That is that Deverell is lying and that I am about to be set up as a guinea-pig to his own design. The metamorphosis may already have begun, but I pray to God it hasn't. No, it is a pessimistic and macabre thought, and I will dismiss it.

Two floors below me, in a room I know better than my own hand, Razzili also waits. He doesn't trust me but he will accompany me tonight for he too knows of no other permutations. It is a pity, for I understand he has a mother in Naples who is very highly strung. Three o'clock. I try to re-read the magazine (it is in French, I have no dictionary) and throw it aside. In my suitcase I find a paperback copy of a popular spy thriller (as if I need such trash, now of all times) that I must have packed by accident. I daydream. I cease, shrug on a mortal coil I discover in a bottom drawer and wait once more. Let me be. Do you not see the notice on my door? I am not to be disturbed. I can't be. Not any more. Concertina the time (light, shadow, twilight, night), dress in a dinner-jacket that stretches over my waist, collect Emilio Razzili, call a taxi, mannequins are about to appear. Let us get this evening over with. I have been waiting in the wings far too long and my motivations, units and objectives strain and jostle to step into the spotlight. First, however, inevitably, the chorus.

*

Someone once said, I forget who, that the model girl's impersonation of rigor mortis during the act of sex no longer amused him. He may well be right, for even though we are in the chandeliered salon of one of Paris's elegant fashion-houses, and the creatures who parade before us still retain their knickers (at least, one trusts they do), their catatonic undulations would baffle Pygmalion. Though I cannot see Medusa among the elite who rim the carpeted plank, applauding each entrance and exit with the enthusiasm of a weasel, I do catch the eye of Melanie and Deverell as they sit, side by side, at the rear of the chairs, constantly in my (and Razzili's) line of vision, except when it is interrupted by the draped bottom (I used the noun with abandon for I have seen smoother contours on a walnut) of the latest creation to be thrust before us. The formula is timeless and the chairs creak. Maxine enters, Maxine's costume is described by a commentator who gives us all the impression that we ought to either throw palms under the girl's feet or canonize her. Maxine pirouettes, Maxine freezes, Maxine returns. Applause, champagne is sipped, catalogue studied, princess and celebrity gawped at, music resumes, no one changes chairs and Angelique enters. I watch as fat women of sixty and bosomy actresses of five-foot-two contemplate buying a two-thousand-dollar dress that is worn by an object weighing seven stone, standing six foot high and with a body like a piece of scaffolding. Little wonder that Razzili and I retire to a corner.

'Can you still see him?' I said.

'Yes, but I can't do it here. Are you mad?'

'There is nowhere else. Once he is outside, he will be sur-rounded. His men are everywhere.'

'But not *here*, Mallory. There are even photographers –'

'Will you listen, Razzili. Two minutes before the show finishes, Deverell will get up and go to the men's washroom over there. It's rather nice, marble and – well, anyway, I am supposed to meet him there in the third cubicle, leaving you alone out here. Then while he is safely out of the way, and the guests leave, you will be suddenly hustled into a waiting car and . . . Are you listening?'

'Yes.'

'So you, not I, join Deverell in the washroom. Don't be embarrassed, he's very normal. And he'll be quite alone.'

Razzili looked at me, then across the room at Deverell and Melanie, sitting unconcerned by a far pillar. A lunar creation, apparently inspired by the latest antics of the astronauts, appears. It is worn by Roxanne, and is beach-wear, entitled 'Endymion's Dream'. One hopes the beach on which she will wear it will be that rather pleasant stretch of sand near the Sea of Tranquillity where it belongs.

'Make up your mind, Razzili. There are three more items only. He'll be getting up in a minute.'

'All right. Where will you be?'

'I'll be at the door. Just in case someone else wants to pass. Go on.'

At that moment, without glancing in our direction, Roland Deverell stood up, placed the catalogue on his chair and walked slowly to the men's washroom in the far corner.

'Cubicle three,' I whispered as Razzili made his way in the semi-darkness behind the unsuspecting observers of Roxanne. I saw the washroom door close, and immediately, as one of Deverell's men moved to guard it, I hurried, as planned, out into the street and into the limousine parked ten yards away. The car didn't move but waited for its owner as I settled in the deep leather, brown leather seats in the back and lit a tipped cigarette.

Although I am not a witness, it is not difficult for me to relate with accuracy the events that are taking place within one part of the brightly lit building on my right. Razzili has entered the washroom, he may even have a gun in his hand, but such details one can embroider for oneself. As Maxine or Janine appears on the boardwalk for the penultimate display, Razzili is pushing open the door of the third cubicle to encounter, not Deverell, but two strangers, far from amiable, who are guiding him in. The door is locked and he is probably now on the ground, cursing me perhaps, struggling as the knives enter, then dying on the blue mosaic tiles to the distant applause for a gorgeous *pièce de résistance* of pink satin and mousseline. His body is now abandoned, the door locked from the inside as the first man stands and leans over its top, then the two men leave, stopping perhaps to wash their hands, comb their hair, steal a drop of Brut, before disappearing into the crowd. Exit Razzili.

A minute later, Melanie appears in the street and enters the car, white-faced.

'Where's Deverell?' I ask.

'He stopped to watch.'

'Well, let us hope he'll buy you a dress. Did you see anything you like?'

Melanie didn't reply, then said quietly :

'They've killed that Italian, haven't they?'

'I expect so,' I replied, offering her a cigarette.

She stared at me, shook her head.

'You're worse than he is, Jay.'

'Yes, I know.'

'But you weren't once.'

'Time passes, Melanie. We all change. Don't we?'

Deverell now appeared smiling, ordered Melanie to sit in the front, closed the door and the partition window, then the car drove off.

'It's a pity, Mallory. He was very good at his job. You know – there was nothing on him. His pockets were empty. Just this.'

He handed me a piece of paper, torn, it appeared, from a diary, on which was written : *C.-D. £5,000.*

'She's paid him less than me,' I said.

'My wife can afford it. You know, I know she hates me but why does she go to all this trouble to kill me? I let her do what she wants, within reason. I give her a generous allowance.'

'I never question the motives of women.'

We were now, I noticed, making for the Champs Élysées and Deverell's hotel, so I leant forward and drew the partition aside.

'Drop me at my hotel first,' I told the chauffeur. 'Quai des Augustins.'

Behind me, Deverell pulled me back.

'Don't stay there. Stay at a decent hotel. I'll give you a suite with me.'

'No, thank you.'

The car then turned right and doubled back and I helped myself to a drink from the bar pocket. A whisky, of course. Through the partition glass, the back of Melanie's head. Surprisingly, after all these years, she was still as beautiful as ever but the light had gone. Not completely, but it was fading.

'I phoned Argyll,' Deverell said quietly. 'She's not there any more.'

'Where is she?'

'Are you sure you want to go through with it?'

'Are you?' I asked.

'No . . . but I won't stop you. A deal is a deal.'

'You sound like Pilate,' I said with a smile.

'Why? Do you think I will betray you?'

'I don't know, but I'll keep it in mind. I have a streak of pessimism in my nature which keeps me alert.'

Deverell grinned, then patted my arm.

'Point taken,' he said.

'Where is she?'

'At Prideau in Brittany. I have a small villa on the beach two miles west of the village. She's certain to be there.'

'Why?'

'Because she flew to France and that's where she'll be. It's very deserted.'

'I'll leave in the morning. After that, you must allow me to retire.'

'You will, Mallory. You will.'

The river was now on our right, cafés on our left, a few cars. I see portents everywhere.

'I want to ask you one favour,' I said.

'What is it?'

'There's a young boy called Atkinson who works for you. Would you fire him, give him a pension, make any excuse, but send him back to the sanity of normal life?'

'Why? Is he no good?'

'He's very good, Deverell. But I don't want him to end up like me. Or even like you. Will you do that?'

'All right. But I'll soon have no employees left.'

'Then you can retire as well.'

The car suddenly stopped and I realized that I was outside my hotel.

'Well,' Deverell said, 'I don't suppose I'll see you again.'

'Who knows?'

'There'll be a black Ford station-wagon outside here in the morning. You'll find everything you need in the boot. Prideau is about a hundred and fifty miles away, due west, if you take the Route Nationale Douze.'

'I'll find it,' I replied, opening the door.

'Good-bye, Mallory.'

Deverell offered his hand but I didn't shake it. Instead I closed the door in his face and was about to enter the hotel when Melanie took my arm:

'Can I stay with you tonight, Jay?'

'No.'

'Why? You always promised me a night in Paris.'

'I'm a married man now, Melanie. Remember?'

I then turned away, seeing Deverell's face staring at me out of the rear window. He looked very tired and very alone.

'Are you sure you won't stay at my hotel? This looks pitiful.'

'Quite sure,' I said. 'Besides, I'm moving my room tonight to the first floor front. It's just been vacated, I understand.'

Ten minutes later, I was lying in the large double bed on the first floor, the windows open, shutters closed. Razzili's briefcase still lay on a chair and an alien suit hung in the wardrobe. But I am in the room at last, as if it were a fortuitous omen of the day in the not-too-distant future when I would be lying beside Celandine once more. My only regret is that, despite finally closing the windows and cutting out the noise, I cannot sleep for four hours. And when I do, it is to dream. I dream I am making love, passionately and agonizingly, making love to this woman under me, above me, before me. But it isn't Celandine who responds to my caresses, screaming, nails tearing my back. It isn't Celandine, nor Melanie nor even Marianne. It is (I alienate the world) my victim, Mrs Celia Deverell.

12. Reunion

When I awoke the next morning, it was to hear the phone ringing in my ears. When I use the word 'ringing', I should be more accurate, for it was an irritating buzzing (accompanied by a flickering light on the face of the dial) that penetrated not only my brain but also my irritation. So I ignored it, dressed quickly and went downstairs. I was in no mood for idle gossip, especially on a day such as this. As I passed the hotel desk, my itinerary was once again interrupted as the clerk called out to me, gesturing to the switchboard:

'Telephone, monsieur.'

'Tell whoever it is that I've already left,' I replied.

'But he insists –'

The words were cut short as I pushed through the swing doors and into the street. The black Ford station-wagon was waiting just outside, key in lock, and I entered and drove off fast with only the anxious face of the clerk signalling to me as he pursued me on foot. Whoever wanted to speak to me would have to wait, wait till the end of the day and then I would talk to the world.

It was a fast car, American, and in this early hour (I glanced at my watch for the first time) the streets of Paris were empty enough for me to be clear of the city within twenty minutes without jumping any lights or endangering any pedestrians. Within a further half an hour, I was in open country, heading west towards the villages of Brittany and the Atlantic beyond. It is difficult to set down in words at this precise moment the feelings in my mind, for to tell you the truth, I had none. An initial nervousness, of course, but that was understandable, but unlike previous assignments, there was no alien hound in my stomach, and my heart-beat, even to the most perceptive cardiologist, was as regular as a metronome. I could well be on my way to the office or to the local supermarket to buy the week-end provisions, for that was how I felt. I saw no landscape, admired no Gothic churches nor acknowledged any benevolent villagers, but merely drove as fast as I could towards my destination. I didn't even daydream.

Once I tried to add up the total number of my victims, and was surprised, like the playboy recalling his mistresses, how few, in fact, they were. All in all, I would hazard that I had killed twenty-five men in twelve years – far fewer than I had been legally responsible for when I was an officer of the Queen – and I can only recall these by the locations of their demise. A seven-acre field in Sussex during the rain while an amateur horseman practised over makeshift jumps and failed the third. The history section of the London Library (dark alley-ways of books, metal catwalks, a copy of Prescott unread in a book-worm's hand), a Pushkin lecture in an Islington church hall, a battery-chicken shed in Surrey with the victim (husband of three) submerged in the sawdust, his body suddenly decorated by a mêlée of chicklets, like parasites on an alligator's back. Others, some more bizarre, as I've betrayed my penchant for exotic arenas once before. Queen Victoria's railway carriage (a sumptuous Pullman, pretty as a lobelia) in Clapham Museum on a half-day. Greenwich amid the decaying uniforms of Nelson. A memorial service for a statesman during which one of the guests met not only his Maker but also his host. A night ferry across the Channel (man over-rash and overboard), a drag club in Berlin. The Colour Television Room in the House of Commons during a Judy Garland musical – I could go on for ever. The subjects, regrettably, I cannot recall, except for one man, on whose cheeks was an acned constellation of spots reminiscent of the Great Bear, who told me he was an un-frocked priest. I had laughed, almost bungling the job, sud-denly struck by the schoolboy thought that the sight of an un-frocked priest is bad enough, but the image of a frocked one can only be farcical. He died in a dress. A gourmet whose wine-cellar was so deep I felt well-advised to bring along a canary. I am now approaching Rennes and the sky is clear.

Before by-passing the town, I stop in a secluded lane, not only to relieve myself, but also to check the contents in the back of the car. Underneath a blanket, I discover a single high-powered rifle, plus sights, in a golfing bag. It is already loaded but with luck I will only need two shots at the most, depending of course on the locale, my own accuracy and the reaction of the victim. You notice I no longer call her by her name for I have erased all such associations from my mind. She is C., that is all. I must think only of the act (and the ten thousand pounds) and nothing more. Anything else, and I might as well give up now. Sandhurst, you see, trains its assassins well. I drive on.

At Ploërmel, with thirty miles to go, I feel I am being followed, for a red Ferrari, as conspicuous as a circus wagon, seems to have been occupying my rear-view mirror for the past ten minutes. It is probably my imagination, but as a precaution I cut away from the main route, double back and continue my journey faster than ever, and alone. By mid-afternoon, I am within sight of Prideau and have parked the Ford in some trees, taken the golfing bag, and am now walking towards the beach.

I see the sea first, the colour of hyacinth, and then the beach, below and to my left, a hundred yards away, no more, and then the villa, set in isolation. From my hide, I can be seen by no one, lying in the tall grass of a sand dune, the rifle now before and under me, butt on shoulder, staring along the barrel at the door of the house for the occupant to appear. There is no one about, except for a group of children a half mile away, a dog, and a boat on the horizon. Otherwise, silence, the sea, a slight breeze. I can only wait, trusting that the sun will encourage the resident of the villa to emerge, and take a walk. She must have eaten by now (one prays she is alone), is unlikely to take a siesta, for she never did at Inverglen, and is not averse, I know, to fresh air. One waits.

I realize I have reflected many times with diminishing nostalgia on memories of Celandine, and while I lie here (cramp is imminent), I suppose I have ample opportunity to recall even more sentimentality, especially as, if Deverell keeps his word, my wife and I will soon be re-united; but I will refrain from further anecdotes, not because I want to spare your feelings but because the door to the villa has opened, the victim, C. (sun highlighting her blonde hair, white loose dress), has appeared and my eye is to the lens of the sight, my finger on the trigger. At first she is in shadow – I hear behind me a car draw up but a distance away – and in the circle of the frame. I focus on her back. She walks, I begin to squeeze the trigger, a voice (male) shouts out to me but the explosion of sound stifles the cry as I fire, the woman spins round, catapults, I see her face, I see her face but I am too well-trained to weaken at that. I see her face and the bullets hurtle towards her, feet run towards me from behind, I hear Deverell calling me to stop, but her forehead is now ripped from her skull and she runs towards the sea as I fire, the rifle ejaculating violently beneath me, a familiar gesture, voices, she falls, calls, enthusiasms, rises, bullets verte-brae her dress, falls, screams, tiger-lilies catch in her throat, she has no face, brains, falls, children run, a beach-ball (red, yellow) bounces to a rock, I am united with the weapon in my hands, firing, obliterating, firing, jerking, thrusting wetly within my hands, a man's voice impeding me, but I am too professional to be distracted by him, by the year broken into smoky panels, she, it, that, blood vomiting in lumps from her mouth as she falls into the surf, legs apart, falls into, falls into the tidewash, respond-ing, her thighs a river, falls into the sea (who is that man with pipe and bowler?), falls, jerks, comes, comes, submerges, shivers and I am spent. Over. Detumescent. I lie still, ex-hausted, my stomach wet, the victim dead. Celandine no more. Celandine. No more . . .

First rule of sniper: Get away from original position as soon as possible. Stay neither to gloat nor mourn. Back away quickly, but I am hindered by this observer who has emerged from a red Ferrari. An enemy? No, I recognize him, stand and salute.

'Mission accomplished, sir. I think we ought to withdraw before we are spotted.'

Deverell stares at me in horror, for he is obviously green to his commission. A crowd of small children, I note, seem to have discovered some debris by the water's edge.

'Mallory, I rang you, pursued you, you must have heard.'

'I repeat, sir, I think we ought to withdraw. Exposed country here, sir.'

'Mallory, I never knew it was Celandine. Believe me. Not until Celia arrived at my hotel this morning.'

He then began to babble on about a brooch (of all things), about someone selling a brooch in order to pay for me. About a message C.-D. £5,000. It's hyphenated,' he tells me. Celandine-Dora not Celia – but I am not one to dither.

'Permission to leave, sir?'

'Mallory – you must have known it was Celandine. You saw her. Why?'

'Can I have my money now, sir?' I say.

'Your money? But your wife is dead. She's lying there –'

'Just the money, sir. With your permission, sir. Just the money, then I'll leave, sir.'

'Money for what? What have you got to live for now? They'll pick you up in a week. Or I will.'

'Just the money, sir. Mission accomplished, sir.'

'Mallory – I never realized your wife loved you so much and hated me so that she wanted –'

'Excuse me, sir, the name is not Mallory, sir. It is Durkin. Easy mistake, sir. Could I have the money, sir. I would like leave.'

'Leave? What leave?'

'Compassionate leave, sir. If I may put in a request for it, sir.'

A woman lies floating in the water, incarnadine. Her face has gone and there are no flowers. She floats like driftwood and what is left of her body is exposed to the elements, unrecognizable except for the lower part of her torso which is angled and stretched, reminiscent of a woman about to give birth to a child. Two men stand a hundred yards away, one at attention, the other turning away to be sick. Sea, children, dog, beach, villa, men, cars, woods, but no more calls. No more enthusiasms. It might be a pageant or a masque. The figures are still, quiet, a slight breeze from the west, a beach-ball returning to rest in a shallow in the sand, like a land-mine, half-covered. A stone pill-box on the hill, the heat of the Arabian sun, no shadows and only the merest glint of light on the polished badges and buckles of the soldiers' uniforms. The soldier at attention is then dismissed, so it appears, and returns to the woods, crouched low, his rifle in one hand, not looking back, while the officer, a younger man, walks to the white, deckle-edged rim of the sea and tenderly picks up the remnants of the casualty of the war. *She has become a pathos – a waif of the tides.* Let us have some darkness.

*

Within a single hour, her absence was opaque. There were no more abstractions. By her bed, the clock remains, silent at ten past three, the ashtray, *The Bell Jar*, the coins, the wedding ring, the book-matches and the cylinder of apple-core now diseased with maggots. A layer of dust has settled on everything around me, on the chair, comb, pillow, even obliterating the disc of white on the bathroom sill, but not yet on the rows of money, stacked in neat piles on the bed. I am alone once more. There are no more violets and the velvet sleeves of her existence have gone for ever. I have not moved for two days, have not slept, have not stirred. I am null. In time, the police will arrive, if the others do not get to me first. But I do not move. I have spread her clothes, her possessions, her life, around me and have bought a figurine. It is here within my sight. No more abstractions. No more assignments. Nothing. Outside, I hear cars drawing up. There is a banging on the front door. Perhaps it is Celandine. She is always forgetting her key. Banging, my name is called, the front door is tried. In time they will try the kitchen door and find it open, for I have unlocked it for them. If only, though, if only before they enter the room I could have the courage, the courage and the strength to move, lean down and pick up her comb. The thread of hair still entwines it and I cannot move. Perhaps, if I imagined it a spider, I could tread on it.

But they enter . . .

Derek Marlowe in Penguins

Do You Remember England?

Who is Dowson? 'When he left on the Sunday – the others had gone to visit Aunt Beth's rose garden (plus *bosquet*) and returned to find his room empty – there were no regrets ... he had stayed thirty-six hours, had glimpsed Hallam's wife only for a second ... and I knew that nothing could ever be the same again.'

Somebody's Sister

No-one needed Walter Brackett any more. He was over the top and had a decade of empty appointment books and silent phones to prove it. Then a fourteen-year-old girl is killed on San Francisco's Golden Gate bridge. She was Brackett's client, and he has a chance to find the killer and rebuild his status in the process.

A Dandy in Aspic

This is the story of a man ordered to Berlin to track down and kill a ruthless Russian assassin and double agent, Krasnevin. A difficult assignment, since he himself is Krasnevin.

Nightshade

A trip to the Caribbean takes Edward and Amy to Haiti, a place of unaccountable fear and peculiar coincidence. Paradise turns to hell, the hell of Baron Samedi, the voodoo lord of death.